TRUTH TIME

"Let's go," Fargo said to the lowlife he had tracked to a mountain cabin. "Some folks have questions for you."

Fargo stepped aside as the man walked toward his horse. "Take the reins and walk him," Fargo said.

The man reached for the reins. Suddenly, in a blur of movement, a gun came from inside his shirt. Fargo dived to his left as the man fired. He hit the ground, rolled, heard another shot slam into the dirt. On his back, Skye fired. The man's body bent over as the heavy slug ripped through his midsection. As he started to go down, his body quivered again as Skye's second shot hit.

Fargo stood up, looked down, and shrugged. He'd have to find somebody else to answer questions . . . or stop bullets . . . or both . . . .

THE
TRAILSMAN
121

REDWOOD
REVENGE

by

Jon Sharpe

A SIGNET BOOK

SIGNET
Published by the Penguin Group
Penguin Books USA Inc., 375 Hudson Street,
New York, New York, 10014, U.S.A.
Penguin Books Ltd, 27 Wrights Lane, London W8 5TZ, England
Penguin Books Australia Ltd, Ringwood, Victoria, Australia
Penguin Books Canada Ltd, 10 Alcorn Avenue, Toronto, Ontario M4V 3B2
Penguin Books (N.Z.) Ltd, 182-190 Wairau Road,
Auckland 10, New Zealand

Penguin Books Ltd, Registered Offices:
Harmondsworth, Middlesex, England

First published by Signet, an imprint of New American Library,
a division of Penguin Books USA Inc.

First Printing, January, 1992

10 9 8 7 6 5 4 3 2 1

The first chapter of this book originally appeared in *Wyoming Manhunt*,
the one hundred nineteenth volume in this series.

 REGISTERED TRADEMARK—MARCA REGISTRADA

PRINTED IN THE UNITED STATES OF AMERICA

The Trailsman

Beginnings . . . they bend the tree and they mark the man. Skye Fargo was born when he was eighteen. Terror was his midwife, vengeance his first cry. Killing spawned Skye Fargo, ruthless, cold-blooded murder. Out of the acrid smoke of gunpowder still hanging in the air, he rose, cried out a promise never forgotten.

The Trailsman they began to call him all across the West: searcher, scout, hunter, the man who could see where others only looked, his skills for hire but not his soul, the man who lived each day to the fullest, yet trailed each tomorrow. Skye Fargo, the Trailsman, the seeker who could take the wildness of a land and the wanting of a woman and make them his own.

1860, the fiercely rugged land of the West Montana Territory, where the only law was the one men made for themselves . . .

1

Nobody wants to be shot dead.

Not anywhere, not any way, not anytime.

But being shot dead in bed is the worst of all, especially in the middle of enjoying a warm and willing woman. It not only robs a man of his life, it robs him of his dignity as well. It adds insult to injury.

These thoughts exploded through Skye Fargo's mind as shots thudded into the bed, flashes of philosophy as unwanted and ill-timed as the sound of the bullets. And now they returned to him once again as he sat beneath the narrow-leaf cottonwood, glad to be alive but filled with anger at how it had all turned out. This was his first chance to let his mind unreel, and he decided to go back over everything that had happened, step-by-step and piece by piece.

He'd start at the beginning—his arrival in town—which suddenly seemed a lot longer than a few short half-dozen hours ago. A letter and a packet of traveling money had brought him to Deerpole. The letter offered the kind of money a man doesn't turn down without a very good reason. And he hadn't any. He'd just finished a job cutting a new trail down Wyoming way and he was happy to go north. He reached Deerpole a day early for his scheduled meeting with the man who had sent the letter, a J. B. Petersen, but he'd only been in town a little while when he felt he already knew something about the man. He was glad for that. It was always better than going into a meeting stone-cold.

It was late afternoon when he arrived in Deerpole and he let his magnificent Ovaro, with its pure white mid-section and jet-black fore-and-hind quarters, slowly walk through the town. The J. B. Petersen Saddlery was the first shop that took his eye. Next he saw the J. B. Petersen Stables and the J. B. Petersen Freight Warehouse. The J. B. Petersen Bank took up a corner near the center of town and another street away he saw the J. B. Petersen General Store. Maybe J. B. Petersen didn't own the whole town, but he was sure a man of influence in it, Fargo concluded with quiet amusement. One of the only structures that didn't carry J. B. Petersen's name was the two-story frame house in the center of town that bore the sign:

DEERPOLE DANCE HALL
DOLLS & DRINKS

The town itself was ordinary enough, he saw, with perhaps a few more Owensboro mountain wagons and dead-axle drays than you'd find in most towns. But then Deerpole nestled alongside the Beaverhead range, where any kind of hauling would require a mountain wagon with oversized brakes. He saw eyes turn to the Ovaro as he rode by, but that always happened in any town he entered. Dusk was beginning to slide across the land when he pulled the Ovaro to a halt in front of a two-story whitewashed building with the sign DEERPOLE INN over the front door. He tethered the horse to a hitching post and strode into the building. Three men lounged in chairs in what passed for a lobby, two half-asleep, hats perched on their heads; the third was a trim figure with a thatch of snow-white hair and very alert gray eyes in a tanned and weathered face.

Fargo halted at the desk, where a middle-aged man with horn-rimmed spectacles and a green eyeshade looked up at him. "Name's Fargo . . . Skye Fargo. I'm here for a meeting with J. B. Petersen," Fargo said. "Anybody come asking for me?"

"Nope," the clerk said.

"I was just wondering. I'm a day early," Fargo said.

"Then you can be sure nobody from Mr. Petersen's will be here till tomorrow," the desk clerk said, a hint of reproach in his tone.

"Stickler for time, is he?" Fargo remarked.

"Some folks call Mr. Petersen Mr. Precision," the clerk said. "Never to his face, of course."

"Then I'll enjoy a soft bed for the night," Fargo said, and the clerk took a key from a row of others on wall pegs and handed it to him.

"Room three, down the hall. That'll be fifty cents," the man said. Fargo slipped the silver coin to him as he took the key. Hurrying outside to the Ovaro, he pulled his saddlebag and pack from the horse and returned to the inn. He walked down the corridor to his room, found it neat and clean with a single bed, a small table with a kerosene lamp on it, a straight-backed chair and a white-pine dresser with a big washbasin atop it. He set his things down, undressed and used the washbasin to freshen up, and finally donned a clean shirt and strolled from the room.

The two half-asleep figures were still in the lobby, but he found the white-haired man standing outside beside the Ovaro. He had a leanness to his trim figure that all but made one forget the thatch of white hair, Fargo thought.

"That's a mighty fine-looking animal you have there," the man said admiringly.

"Thank you. That makes you a good judge of horseflesh." Fargo smiled.

"Been at it for enough years," the old man said.

"You as good a judge of a place to eat?" Fargo queried.

"At the dance hall, best food in town," the man answered. "And you can kill two birds with one stone."

Fargo's brows lifted. "Meaning what?"

"Meaning I didn't wait around just to compliment you on that Ovaro," the man said. "Been waiting for days for you to show up. I've a message for you."

"Who from?" Fargo frowned. "I don't know anybody in this town."

"From Evie. You can find her at the dance hall. She works there," the man said.

Fargo nodded. "Two birds with one stone," he said and it was the old man's turn to nod. "Who the hell is Evie?"

"Somebody who wants to see you."

"You can do better than that," Fargo said.

The old man shrugged. "Not much," he said.

"What does Evie want with me?"

"That's for her to tell you."

"What does she look like?"

"Ask for Dolly. She runs the place. She'll point Evie out to you," the old man told him.

"What if I don't go? I'm not big on strange messages," Fargo said, his eyes hard on the old man.

"Then I've wasted three days waiting around."

"How did this Evie know I'd be coming into town?" Fargo pressed.

The old man half snorted. "Word gets around," he said. He was good with cryptic answers, Fargo grunted silently. But his curiosity had been aroused, and he unwound the reins from the hitching post.

"As you said, I'm going over for a meal anyway," he remarked.

"I'll walk over with you," the man said, and fell into step beside Fargo.

"Where do you fit in?" Fargo questioned.

"I just carry messages."

"Bullshit, friend," Fargo said blandly, and the old man allowed himself a small shrug.

"I know Evie. We're old friends," he conceded.

"You've a name," Fargo said.

"Most folks call me Nugget."

"Old miner?"

"One who never struck it rich."

"You've plenty of company there," Fargo säid, casting another glance at the man. His smallish, trim body held together well, but there were a myriad of tiny red veins in the weathered face that sent their own message. "You mine for whiskey bottles now," he said, and saw the man's quick glance of surprise.

"You judge a man real quick, Fargo," Nugget said.

"Usually real good," Fargo replied and drew a snort

and nothing more until they reached the dance hall where the square stream of yellow light reached from the swinging doors into the night.

"You're on your own from here, Fargo," Nugget said.

"Afraid of temptation or afraid of being thrown out?" Fargo smiled.

"Some of both," the old man admitted wryly. "Good luck."

Fargo wondered how much the old man really knew. Or was he no more than he'd claimed to be, simply a messenger? "Where could I find you?" he asked.

"A shack, north end of town," the man said. "But you won't have any need to find me. Just talk to Evie."

"How come you and Evie are friends?" Fargo pressed.

Nugget shrugged as he thought for a moment. "Misery likes company, maybe," he said as he hurried away.

Fargo turned and pushed his way through the two swinging doors into the dance hall. It was the usual place of its kind—a long bar, smoke-filled air, and round tables along three sides of the big room. And girls in black-net tights, most of them with form-fitting satin tops, some dancing with patrons, others seated at the tables. They were the usual also, girls grown old too quickly, every smile a mask. He moved forward, his eyes sweeping the dance hall again. A stairway at the back led to the second floor, and he spotted a woman at a corner table near it. She was some thirty pounds overweight, part of it makeup and the jewelry that hung from her wrists and neck.

She had a round face with an extra chin, tightly curled bottle-blond hair, and false eyelashes. But he saw none of the harshness in her face that many dance hall madams wore. Her eyes darted around the room more like a watchful mother hen's than a taskmistress's. Her gaze

14

settled on him as he strolled to her table, instant approval in her appraisal. "Hello, big man," she said in a throaty voice.

"You Dolly?" he asked.

"In person. What'll it be, drinks, dolls or both?"

"A good meal first," Fargo said as he slid into a chair.

The woman snapped her fingers and one of the girls hastened over. "Bring the man a buffalo sandwich and lots of gravy," Dolly said.

"And a bourbon. No bar whiskey," Fargo added.

"You heard the man," Dolly said, and Fargo watched the woman's eyes appraise him again. "I've some real nice girls for afterward," she said.

"I've one in mind," Fargo told her and drew a glance of surprise.

"You've never been here before," Dolly said.

"That's right."

"Ah, somebody recommended a special girl."

"Something like that." Fargo smiled. The strange message had surprised him. The old man had been cryptic. He'd keep things the same way for now, Fargo decided, and exchanged small talk with the madam until the girl returned with his food and a bourbon. He sipped the whiskey. "Good," he said nodding approvingly at the madam.

"Everything we have here is good, mister," she said. She sat back with a faintly amused smile, watching as he finished the meal and downed the last of the bourbon. "Now who's this special girl you want?" she asked.

"Evie," he said, and watched the woman's plucked eyebrows shoot upward.

"Evie?" she echoed, disbelief in her voice.

"That so surprising?" Fargo questioned.

"It sure as hell is, especially from a handsome gent like you," the madam said. "Evie's only been here for a few weeks, and nobody's taken to her. She's just not the type for this kind of work. I told her so."

"Why'd you take her on?"

"Because I'm a sucker for stray cats," the woman said. "There was some big breakup with a boyfriend who took off. Then she was fired from her job at the general store. Some of my girls knew her from there."

"And told her to come to you for a job," Fargo said.

"She seemed awfully nervous and afraid when she came. I think she was looking for anyplace she could feel safe. I told her I'd take her on trial. I knew she wasn't going to work out."

"But you felt sorry for her," Fargo said.

"I told you, I'm a sucker for stray cats."

"I've heard of worse things to be," Fargo said, and let his eyes move across the room. "Which one is she?" he asked.

"She's upstairs. I keep her there till later," Dolly said.

"Why?"

"The customers. The more they drink the less particular they are," she said, and Fargo smiled. "You think I'm being callous?" she said.

"Nobody's perfect," Fargo said. "You have the right. Is she that bad?"

"No, she's just not the kind my customers take to," the madam said. She paused and her eyes narrowed at him. "But you're not my average customer. Nobody recommended her to you. Something else brought you here looking for her," she said.

"Maybe." He shrugged and the woman gave a little

grunt, pleased at her own perceptiveness. She called another of the girls over.

"Go and tell Evie to come down here," she said, and the girl hurried to the stairs as Fargo sat back. Dolly exchanged banter with a few passing patrons while Fargo's eyes stayed on the stairs. He had no need to question Dolly when the girl came down the stairs. She wore the black-net stockings all the other girls wore, but she was slightly built, her red satin top covering plainly small breasts. He watched her approach him, her eyes round, a light blue. She had a wan, waiflike quality to her that evoked his instant protectiveness.

"Nugget sent me," he murmured softly, and her round eyes grew rounder.

"You're Fargo," she said, and he nodded. "Come upstairs with me," she said, and he rose as she turned. He cast a glance at Dolly and saw the woman watching him uncertainly.

He threw her a smile. "One more good deed," he said and she tossed a glance of grim patience back. But she turned away and he laughed softly as he followed the girl up the stairs. Dolly had a good heart under all that paint and powder. He reached the upstairs corridor just a step behind Evie and saw a dim passageway with kerosene lamps shaded by deep red glass to make the hall even dimmer. Evie halted at a door near the end of the corridor, opened it, and admitted him to a small room all but filled by a big bed and a straight-backed chair. A narrow bureau took up the only remaining wall space.

A lamp turned low offered a dim yellow glow as Evie sat down on the edge of the bed. "Thanks for coming," she said, her small, thin voice matching her waiflike appearance. He wanted to be brusque and annoyed—he'd every reason to be, he told himself—yet he couldn't manage it. With no attempt to manipulate, she had a disarming air to her, he realized.

"What's this all about, Evie?" he asked gently.

"It's about a favor I'm asking," she said. "I know why you're here. I don't want you to kill Burt."

Fargo frowned at her. "I'm here because I got a letter about a job," he said.

The girl's smooth forehead creased. "That's all you know?" she asked.

"Yes, that's all," Fargo snapped. "Maybe you should tell me the rest, seeing as you seem to know so much."

She frowned in thought for a moment. "I don't know if I should," she said. "Anyway, I want to talk about our agreement first."

"About my not killing Burt?"

"That's right." She nodded.

"First, who's Burt?" she asked.

"He was my boyfriend."

"The one who ran away," Fargo said, and saw the surprise flash in her pale blue eyes. "Dolly mentioned it," he added.

"He had to run," the girl said.

"Why would I want to kill him?" Fargo questioned.

"It might just happen and I don't want that, so I want to make our bargain first," Evie said.

"Such as?"

"I'll pay you not to kill Burt, only I don't have any money right now," she said. "You can have me instead. Now, tomorrow, when you come back—anytime, anywhere, as often as you like."

She halted, waiting, and he studied the wan face that had suddenly taken on a determination that seemed out of place in it. "Burt must be quite a guy," Fargo said.

She offered a wry smile. "I may never see him again, but he was good to me when I needed someone. He did a lot for me. Now it's my turn. That's the way I am."

Fargo's smile was gentle as he continued to study her. "Maybe you're quite a young woman," he said, words that were more than a glib compliment. There was a quiet strength behind her waiflike surface.

She shrugged. "It's something I want to do," she said, her blue eyes focusing on him as he continued to study her. She suddenly rose to her feet. "Maybe I'm not all that beautiful, but you'll enjoy it, I promise," she said, a touch of defensiveness in her voice.

"Wasn't thinking about that," Fargo said.

"You were thinking about something."

"I was thinking I'd best find out more about why I'm here and how it involves your friend Burt."

"He'd be a side issue, but he could still get killed, and that's what I don't want to happen," Evie said.

"Maybe I can see that that doesn't happen. I don't know. I don't know much of anything. But there'll be no bargaining with you for it," Fargo said.

A tiny furrow moved across her smooth forehead as she fastened him with a sidelong glance filled with skepticism. "You saying you'd do what I want with nothing between us?"

"Guess so," he grunted.

"Why?" Evie asked, the furrow deepening.

He shrugged. "That's the way I feel. Consider it a

19

present. Everybody makes their own choices about what's right and what's wrong.''

The furrow became a full frown. ''No, I wouldn't ask that. It wouldn't be fair,'' she said.

''Don't look a gift horse in the mouth, honey,'' Fargo told her.

''No, it'd be wrong. I've my own ideas about what's right and what's wrong. We make a bargain and seal it here and now. I want an agreement, not charity,'' Evie said firmly.

Fargo's lips tightened in a grim half-smile. She had her own stubborn integrity. Maybe it was skewed, but it was there and she'd cling to it, he realized. Once again, another facet of her elfin appeal reached out to him. ''One condition,'' he said. ''You tell me everything you know about why I'm here.''

''All right, but afterward. We seal it first. I don't want you changing your mind,'' she said.

''How do you know I won't do that anyway, afterward?''

''You won't do that. You're not that kind. I can tell,'' she said.

''You that good a judge of men?'' He laughed.

''Inside things,'' she said with a lofty simplicity that he understood all too well. She took a step backward, unsnapped the buttons at the bottom of her red top, slid the black-net stockings from her legs with graceful, quick motions, and then undid another pair of hooks and the top fell from her. She stood before him with a kind of defiant pride, as if daring him to disparage her with a glance or expression. He'd no mind to do that anyway, but she would have pushed it aside if he'd had the urge. The waiflike quality in her face echoed faintly in her body, yet she had a surprising sensuality. His eyes moved down a slim, girlish form with small breasts, slightly flat, tipped by tiny pink nipples.

A lean, trim body, small-waisted, good hips and a flat belly, and just beneath it a surprisingly thick black nap. Her legs, on the thin side, but shapely, with thighs that were long and inviting. She sat down on the bed, lay back on her elbows, and the blue eyes shone with a tiny flickering fire. She was, he decided, a strange combination of waif and wanton hussy—little-girl appeal and very womanly sensuality, a mixture of contrasts both physical and emotional. Her flat little breasts with their pink nipples enticed him as she lay waiting. She drew one leg up with slow provocativeness.

He undid his gunbelt, let it slide to the floor, and followed with his clothes. He felt himself already responding to her. When he stood naked before her he saw her eyes fasten on him and the tiny flicker suddenly grew into a pale fire. He lowered himself atop her gently. She was small to the touch, his hand almost encompassing her ribs on one side, but he felt her body quiver as their skins met. "What if I'd been a fat, ugly old fossil?" he asked. "Would you still have gone through with it?"

"I don't know. That honest enough for you?" she answered, and he nodded. "Probably," she added. "But I'd have hated everything about it."

"And now?"

"I don't think I'm going to hate anything," Evie murmured. Her mouth opened for his lips and he felt her thin arms come up to wrap around his neck. Her tongue was quick, darting out to meet his, her mouth softly drawing him in as she murmured a sigh. His hands found one small breast and gently caressed the tiny pink tip, felt it harden and grow a fraction higher. He pulled his mouth from hers, drew his lips down her neck to the other breast, and pulled it into his oral embrace. He let his tongue circle the tiny tip and Evie's little murmured sound grew stronger, became a thin cry of delight. He felt her body move, half-twist one way, then the other, stretch itself out, and he let his hand slide down over the flat abdomen and push into the thick nap. He closed his fingers gently in the denseness, the soft filaments wrapping around his fingers as he massaged the little Venus mound. "Yes, Jesus, yes. . . ." Evie whispered and again he felt her body stretch out.

Her hips lifted, her small frame suddenly finding a wiry strength as he felt her thighs grow muscled. His hand slipped from the dense black nap, smoothed the flesh of her slim thighs, and moved upward, cupping around the moist and secret places. Evie gave a short cry of delight as he touched deeper. Her hands made fluttering little motions along his back, little exhortations of touch, and her hips rose in a tiny boucing movement. Her thin body half-twisted again and the small breasts moved from side to side. He felt himself responding and her hands were against his buttocks, pulling him atop her. She gave a little cry as his throbbingness came against the dense nap. "Yes, yes, Jesus, yes . . ." she gasped out as her thighs fell wide apart and she made the tiny, bouncing motion with her hips again.

He was just bringing himself to her waiting openness when he heard the loud snap of the door being flung open, crashing against the wall, the sound as jarring as it was unexpected. Still atop Evie, about to slide forward to her, he turned his head to see three men burst into the room, all with six-guns in their hands. His own gun lay on the floor between the bed and the intruders, too far away to reach without being blasted. There was a narrow space between the other side of the bed and the wall, hardly more than a foot and a half. He rolled from atop Evie, flung himself into the space as, with one hand, he yanked her with him. He had her almost pulled into the space when the trio opened fire.

"Aw, shit," Fargo groaned, feeling Evie's body shudder as the shots thudded into her. "Goddamn son of bitches!" he shouted as he rose, fury throwing aside prudence. Two more bullets slammed into Evie. Fargo dived across the bed, hit the other side, and somersaulted to the floor. He had his hand on the Colt as the three men turned and began to streak for the door. He got the gun up fast enough to fire one shot at the last of the three figures, saw the man clutch at the back of his leg before he disappeared from sight.

Fargo leaped to his feet, raced forward to see the man dragging himself into the corridor. "Stop!" he shouted, and saw the man turn and bring his gun up. Fargo fired, and this time the man clutched at his midsection as he flew backward and hit the wall. Fargo ran past his body as it slid to the floor. The other two men were almost to the end of the corridor. One of the two looked back for an instant. "Down the stairs, Jack," he said, words clipped out with an accent that was German or maybe Swedish.

"I'm goin'," the other said in a very throaty, husky voice. Both disappeared down the stairs as Fargo raced forward, hit the top step, and leaped down the next three and the three that followed. He heard the rising shouts of alarm as the main room of the dance hall appeared in front of him. Customers and girls ducked and flattened themselves on the floor as the two gun-waving figures raced across the room. "Out of the way, goddamnit!" one shouted in his throaty voice, and Fargo cursed as he aimed the Colt. A fat man got in the way as he drew a bead on the man with the accent. He shifted his aim to the other one only to see two of the girls come into his sight.

"Damn!" he swore as he aimed the gun and fired just as the men reached the doorway. His shot sent a shower of wood splinters from the door. Both men raced out of the dance hall and Fargo lowered the Colt. He saw the madam huddled in one corner staring up at him. So were all the other eyes in the room, and it was only then that he realized he was stark-naked. He retreated up the stairs, turned and ran back to the room, where he swore softly as he dived onto the bed and reached down to pull Evie from the narrow space. He had felt the bullets thud into her thin body and he'd held no hope for a miracle, but he swore again as he found himself too right. He held Evie's small form in his arms, rocked her for a long moment before he put her down on the bed.

He rose, his chest covered with blood from her wounds, and had just drawn on his trousers when Dolly came into the room, the bartender and a man with a sheriff's badge on his vest following her. She looked down at Evie and he heard her sob. "Oh, God," she breathed, and brought her gaze up to Fargo's bitter, angry eyes. "What happened?"

"You tell me," he bit out. "Didn't you see them go by you, damnit?"

"I saw them go upstairs. I didn't think anything of it. Sometimes the girls make arrangements they tell me about later. Then I heard the shooting," Dolly said. "Evie didn't have any enemies. They had to be after you."

"I figured that out myself," Fargo snapped. "I just don't know why."

"What's your name, mister?" the man with the badge asked. "I'm Sheriff Hood."

"Fargo, Skye Fargo. I came for a meeting with J. B. Petersen."

"You're the one," the sheriff grunted.

"Jesus, everybody in this town knows about me coming here?" Fargo asked.

"Wouldn't say everybody, but there's been talk," the sheriff said.

"Enough to have three hired guns come after me," Fargo threw back acidly. "And I don't know a damn reason why."

"I don't know that either, mister," the man said.

"But I'll bet you could take a guess."

"I don't gamble and I don't guess," the sheriff said, and leaned out into the corridor. "I'll send Jake to haul this one away," he told Dolly as he left.

The woman turned to Fargo. "I'll see to Evie. Hell, you just met her. It's my place to take care of things."

"A man gave me her message to come see her. Called himself Nugget. Seems they were friends," Fargo said.

"Yes, old Nugget. I'll see that he hears, though somebody will tell him before I do," Dolly said with another quick glance at the bed. "I'll take care of her good and proper, Fargo."

He reached into his pocket and handed her a dozen bills. "Get her a real headstone," he said.

Dolly nodded. "I'll send a girl with water and towels for you," she said, and hurried from the room. He lowered himself to the edge of the bed beside the small, still form, and his hand was still stroking her hair when the girl arrived with the towels and a large washbasin. She helped him clean himself off before he put on the rest of his clothes.

The saloon was a strangely subdued place when he went downstairs, half the customers gone. He strode out into the night. His lips were a thin line as he unhitched the Ovaro. It had become damn obvious that the offer that had brought him here to Deerpole had all kinds of dirty strings attached to it. And too many people knew about those strings. He couldn't claim anything so profound as betrayal. He couldn't even claim he'd been misled. The letter had neither promised nor implied. But he had just been damn near killed, and that deserved an answer. And a young woman lay dead, and she deserved justice.

J. B. Petersen was suddenly more than a name at the bottom of a letter in his pocket. It was a question mark that needed an answer. With cold anger seething inside him, he climbed onto the Ovaro. He'd paid for a room and a soft bed at the inn. But he had been trailed to Evie. Maybe others were lying in wait at the inn. He decided not to risk another dry-gulching. He could pick up his things in the morning. He turned the horse south and rode from town, finally climbing a low hill until he found the big cottonwood. Now he turned off his thoughts and closed his eyes.

Evie's slender form and sweet, wan face drifted through his mind. Hell, he'd never even learned her last name, he realized. He went to sleep wrapped in grim anger he knew would be no less grim when the new day dawned.

2

When morning came he decided to find the white-haired old man first, and he made a circle around town to approach it from the north. He spotted a tumbledown shack a few hundred yards from the outskirts of town, halted before it, and swung to the ground. A door hung open, balanced precariously from one hinge, and he stepped into the shack to peer through the dimness. A clutter of old cardboard boxes, crates, and battered steamer trunks met his eyes, but he saw light from a side window in a second room. He stepped toward it, pushed his way past more crates, and saw a cracked table and a mattress on the floor. The trim white-haired figure swung around on the mattress to sit up. Fargo saw the half-empty whiskey bottle in the man's hand.

"Breakfast as usual or did you hear?" Fargo asked coldly.

"I heard," Nugget said, made an effort to get up, and fell back on the mattress. Fargo studied the weathered face and decided the man was still sober enough to make sense.

"Talk to me," Fargo snapped.

"Don't know anything. Told you that last night."

"Who tried to kill me last night?"

"I don't know."

"Don't lie to me," Fargo warned.

"I don't know. Honest, I don't," the old miner said.

Fargo reached down, closed one hand around the front of the man's shirt, and lifted him into the air. "Guess," he rasped.

"I don't know. Ask Petersen."

Fargo opened his hand and the man fell back onto the mattress. He kept his hold on the bottle, Fargo noted. "You were friends with Evie. What'd she tell you?" he asked.

"Only that she had to see you," Nugget said.

"How did she figure into it?" Fargo pressed.

"She didn't. The boyfriend worked for Petersen. That's all I know," the man insisted.

Fargo swore silently. He was wasting time. Maybe Nugget knew more. Maybe he didn't. Maybe he was too afraid to talk. Or maybe he just hid in whiskey, old habits too deep to change. Fargo turned and pushed his way through the rubble. He'd turn to another place. He rode the Ovaro through Deerpole to the inn, halted and dismounted, his eyes sweeping the street as a matter of precaution. When he went into the inn the desk clerk beckoned to him.

"Gent waiting for you," he said, and Fargo stepped into the lobby to see a long-legged cowhand there.

"I'm Fargo," he said.

"Come to take you to the Petersen place," the cowhand told him.

"I'll get my things and see you outside," Fargo said, and strode to the room. He retrieved his pack and saddle-bag and carried them to the Ovaro, where the cowhand waited atop a long-maned quarter horse. Fargo tied his things in place and followed the man at a leisurely pace across land that rose into low hills heavy with box elder and bur oak. Suddenly the land dipped to become a dishlike hollow with the buildings in its center—a big log-and-frame main house with a low roof, two long cow barns, a stable, and a bunkhouse. In a distant corral he saw some fifty steers. "Petersen is a rancher as well as owner of most of the town," Fargo commented to his guide.

"Petersen is everything and anything," the cowhand said as they drew up in front of the main house. "Go on in. They're waiting for you inside," he said, and Fargo dismounted and walked to the flagstone entrance to the house. The tall, dark oak door was ajar. He pushed it all the way open and stepped into a large room where thick scatter rugs covered the floor and tapestries hung from the walls. Heavy, dark furniture filled the room, and in the center was a heavy, dark desk, a man seated behind it and a woman standing beside him.

Fargo walked to the desk, a journey of more than a few steps, and felt his brow crease. The man sat in a wheelchair. He was gaunt of face with graying hair combed straight back, a thin nose, and a thin-lipped mouth that turned down at the corners. He sat motionless and stared straight ahead through watery blue eyes, and Fargo saw that his hands were clenched around the arms of the wheelchair. He seemed lifeless except for the soft rasp of breath that came through the thin lips. Fargo's eyes went to the woman and saw a tall, strong figure, wide-shouldered and

29

full-hipped with breasts that filled the top of a dark green cotton dress with a square neck that showed the swell of soft curves.

Her almost blond hair, pulled back and held by a bone clip, gave a slightly severe cast to an attractive face with a long, delicate nose, wide cheekbones, and lips that were almost perfectly molded with sharp edges. Gray-blue eyes seemed cool yet simmered with a deep fire. She was perhaps thirty, he guessed, certainly no more, a very well-proportioned, statuesque figure. She offered a sudden smile that was fashioned of cool control and appraisal.

"Good morning, Fargo," she said in a soft, well-modulated voice. She rested one hand on the man's shoulder. "This is J. B. Petersen," she said. The man in the wheelchair didn't move as he continued to stare straight ahead. "He had a stroke," she said.

"Can he see?" Fargo asked.

"Yes, and he can hear. But he can't speak and he can barely move."

"How soon after he sent for me?" Fargo queried.

"Before he sent for you," she answered. Fargo saw her enjoy his frown, a tiny smile edging her molded lips.

"Then who sent the letter?" he asked.

"I did. I'm J. B. Petersen," she said.

Fargo's eyes hardened. "You want to stop playing games, honey," he growled.

"No games. This is my father, James Benton Petersen. I'm Joanna Barbara Petersen," she said. Lifting her hands, she gave a single sharp clap. A smallish man wearing a white servant's jacket over dark trousers appeared from a side door, immediately went to the wheelchair and stood behind it. Joanna Petersen came around the desk, her statuesque body moving with grace. She halted in front

30

of Fargo, cool approval in her quick appraisal. "We've a lot to talk about, Fargo," she said.

"You're damn right," he snapped. "I almost had my head blown off last night."

"At the dance hall. I heard," Joanna Petersen said. "We can talk about that later. I want to tell you why I sent for you." The servant wheeled J. B. Petersen out of the room and Joanna led the way to a thick, leather sofa and sank down on it, the fabric across the top of her dress pulling tight with the movement of her full breasts.

She motioned to Fargo and he sat down beside her. "I want you to find a man. I've some leads where he may have gone, and I need someone to track him down. Double your usual fee," she said.

"What's his name?"

"Duncan Kale."

"Why do you want him tracked down?"

"He was my father's partner for twenty years. Then he just up and took off. That's when we found most of the money was gone."

"He'd taken it," Fargo finished.

"Not all at once. He'd never have gotten away with that. He had to have been doing it for years, which we found out was exactly what he'd been doing. He'd been juggling the books, faking deposits, falsifying ledgers, and siphoning off money every week."

"Your pa never had any suspicions?"

"My father was always too busy making deals, buying new businesses, expanding the ones he already had. He trusted Duncan implicitly with everything that had to do with the books. He had no idea. Duncan planned long and carefully."

"What if I find Duncan Kale?"

"I want him alive if at all possible. I want all that money back," Joanna said. "He has it someplace."

"And after you find it?"

She fell silent for a moment. "It wouldn't bother me any to see him dead, I'll admit," Joanna said finally, and her calm voice suddenly took on an edge. "You find him. I'll see to everything else."

"Seems you talked plenty about hiring me," Fargo said.

"Word just gets around."

"Enough to get me killed in the dance hall."

"That's the price of patronizing such places," she said with lofty dismissal.

Fargo's smile was chiding. "You can get a lot of things at such places. You can get cheated, rolled, beaten up, drunk and the clap, but not usually gunned down in bed."

"There's a first time for everything," she said with no change in the loftiness.

"Somebody knew I'd be there and sent three varmints to kill me," Fargo growled.

"Obviously Duncan Kale, to stop you from helping me," Joanna said.

"He had to know," Fargo persisted.

"As I said, word just gets around," she returned.

"And a young girl is dead because of it," Fargo said. "Somebody's going to pay for that."

"Now you've another reason to go after Duncan Kale," Joanna said. She was quick to seize an opening and he could admire that. But Evie's death had evoked only her passing sympathy and he couldn't admire that.

"Who's Burt?" he thrust at her, and the gray-blue eyes narrowed for an instant.

"Burt Dimmons. He worked for my father as an

32

assistant to Duncan. He ran off when Kale did," she said. "How'd you know his name?"

"Evie told me," Fargo answered.

"She tell you anything else?"

"She would have. She never got the chance," Fargo said, and felt instant anger boil up inside him.

"Too bad," Joanna said, and again the words were only that. She saw his eyes hard on her. "Maybe she could've told you something to help," Joanna said quickly. He shrugged, accepted the explanation. Joanna rose, unfolding herself to stand very straight, her statuesque beauty commanding. "Do we have an agreement? Will you track Duncan Kale down for me?"

He considered the practical aspect of her offer—money a man would be a fool to turn from. It was enough of a reason, but she was right. He had another reason now. Duncan Kale had sent the trio of killers after him. The man would pay. "You've got a deal," he said.

Her smile was quick, surprisingly bright and appealing, all the reserved coolness exploded away in a flash. She pressed her hand over his, a quick, unplanned gesture drawn back just as quickly.

"You won't be sorry, Fargo," she said.

"Where does your pa fit into all this?"

"I'll tell him. I run all the J. B. Petersen enterprises since his stroke. Decisions are mine," she said. "When do you start?"

"Tomorrow. Time's not crucial. I'll be following the cold trail of a man long gone."

"I've some leads, I told you," she said.

"Everything helps," Fargo said. "I'll have a lot of questions for you tomorrow."

She walked to the tall oak door with him, watched him swing onto the Ovaro. He turned to look back at her as he began to ride away. She let the almost blond hair loose and it cascaded down to frame her face. It didn't change her statuesque beauty, but it softened it a little. He rode on out of the dish of land, taking note of landmarks. The day had moved into mid-afternoon when he circled Deerpole again to come into the town from the north. He dismounted and pushed his way into the shack, stumbling past wooden crates to the second room, where he saw the trim figure seated on the mattress just below the window.

The bottle lay beside him as Nugget looked up and Fargo saw that it was still only half empty. His shrug conceded surprise as it questioned. "There's no hiding from some things," Nugget said.

"Good," Fargo agreed. "I met with Joanna Petersen and she told me about Duncan Kale and tracking him down."

"So what brings you back here?" The old miner glowered. "You know it all now."

"I know what she told me. I want to hear what you have to say," Fargo said. "You hear. You listen. It's time for you to talk. How'd you know Evie?"

"She was good to me. She was always a kind of lone sparrow, always on the outside of things. But she wouldn't take charity. She had her own standards. We used to have long talks about being on the outside."

"Birds of a feather," Fargo said.

Nugget nodded. "You could say that."

"What about this Burt Dimmons?" Fargo asked.

"He was good to her. I think he really cared about her."

"He still ran with Duncan Kale," Fargo commented.

"When a man's sucked in too deep he sometimes has no choice but to run," the old miner answered.

"Guess so," Fargo agreed. "But it seems plain enough that Kale sent that murdering pack to stop my helping Joanna Petersen."

"Probably," Nugget said, the word guarded, and Fargo frowned.

"What's that mean?" he asked.

"It means it probably was Kale, like you said, but a lot of folks could've hired them," Nugget said.

"Why?"

"To help Kale in their own way, and for revenge," Nugget said. "J. B. Petersen is a rotten, stinking bastard. He ran roughshod over everybody in this town, forced folks out of business, cheated and lied and strong-armed his way into becoming a powerful man. A lot of people hate him. They'd be happy to stop you, or anybody, from helping Petersen. They feel he got what he deserved."

"I don't buy that as an excuse to come trying to kill me," Fargo said coldly.

"Didn't expect you would. You asked and I answered," Nugget said. "Chances are it was Kale who had those varmints waiting." He paused, pulled himself to his feet, and stared out the grimy window. "They're burying Evie tomorrow," he said, his voice heavy. "Life never gave her a fair shake. Maybe it was meant to be."

"Somebody ought to pay. I'll see they do," Fargo said, and the old miner turned to fasten a long glance at him.

"Those are good words, Fargo," Nugget said. "Enough to make a man stay sober."

"Give it a try," Fargo said, and saw the old miner frown for a moment, then toss the half-empty bottle into a corner before he sank back down onto the mattress. Fargo turned and made his way from the shack and outside, saw the dark beginning to slip over the land. He climbed onto the pinto, rode slowly, and halted at the Deerpole Dance Hall as night fell. He thought about going in and decided against it. He'd nothing to say and no stomach for the place and he moved the horse forward.

But out of the corner of an eye he thought he saw movement in the black shadows across the street along the building line. The Colt seemed to leap into his hand as he peered into the darkness, hunched over the saddlehorn, ears as well as eyes straining, but he saw no movement. The passages between the buildings were pitch-black and he sent the horse forward in a slow walk. The Colt stayed in his hand until he reached the end of town and dropped it back into its holster. He rode into the hills at a slow, deliberate pace, glancing back into the trees with casual frequency. But there was hardly a sliver of moon and he saw nothing but the night blackness. Perhaps it was only his own edginess, the aftermath of the attempted dry-gulch, he told himself as he rode deeper into the hills.

But the uneasiness clung, a feeling of being followed. He finally found a low-branched shadbush that melted into the surrounding trees. He dismounted, unsaddled the horse, and decided against a fire, though the night had turned cool. He slid down with his back against the smooth gray-brown bark and ate a strip of dried beef from his saddlebag. When he finished, he put his head back and let his eyes close—but not in sleep, not yet. Instead, he let the night sounds surround him, forming their own pattern made up of droning, clicking, and buzzing noises. He listened, let the pattern of sound paint its own picture. If he had been followed, there was no more than one pursuer. He'd have picked up more than one. And that one, if he existed at all, was damn cautious and keeping a good distance.

Fargo continued to relax and listen. When the night remained unchanged, no sudden scrape or cracking twig to disturb the auricular pattern, he relaxed and let sleep begin to wrap itself around him. He felt confident. The night was inky blackness and he was encased in it. No one could target him from a distance and he knew no one could creep close enough to fire without waking him. Like the great mountain cats, a part of him was never completely asleep. He settled down more comfortably and slept.

The night brought nothing to interrupt his slumber and he opened his eyes with the first gray light of dawn. He remained motionless and listened, one hand resting on the butt of the Colt at his side. Only the morning birdsongs came to him, Bullock orioles to his right, black-capped chickadees to the left, with the deeper call of horned larks mixed in. Another sound came to him, the soft murmur of a woodland brook some yards away. He hadn't picked it up during the night, probably because it hadn't been running as swiftly. Many wood brooks, fed by high water, pick up speed and flow with the sun and slow down with the night. He stood up, took soap and a towel from his saddlebag, and walked a dozen yards deeper into the trees, where he found the brook.

It grew noisier as he reached it, skipping and slapping its way over a bed of small stones. Dropping to his knees, he took the Colt from his holster, and placed it on the ground beside him where it would be quick to reach while he was bent over the stream. He bent low, cupped his hand, and brought the clear, cool water to his face. He had just finished washing when the tranquility of the woods shattered with the blast of a shot. He started to grab for the gun and saw the bullet smash into the ground a fraction from the Colt. The force of the shot sent the gun skittering along the bank of the stream. He started to scramble after it only to dive sideways as another bullet smashed into the ground inches from his shoulders. He rolled into the stream and came out on the other side as a third shot barely missed hitting him; it threw up a spray of water.

He kept rolling into a line of brush and stayed low. The shooter was reloading, he was certain as he peered through the leaves and stalks of the brush. He reached one hand out, shook a section of brush, and the bullet came at once, slamming into the brush as he rolled in the other direction. He kept rolling until he was opposite the Colt where it lay just across the stream. He halted, realizing he hadn't drawn any more shots. Rifle fire, he grunted, and gauged the distance to the gun. He'd have to distract the shooter to have any chance of making it to the Colt, he realized, his gaze sweeping the trees. Nothing moved and he stayed motionless himself, his lips pulling back in a grimace. A deadly cat-and-mouse game had developed, with himself as the mouse, a role he didn't particularly fancy.

His glance swept the suddenly still woods again. The first shots had come from somewhere to his left and he guessed the shooter was still there. Fargo's eyes went to the Colt again. The gun had skittered a dozen or more feet along the stream and he wondered again if he might just be able to reach it. He might if the shooter was looking for him in the brush a dozen yards to the left. Fargo swore. He knew he wanted to try even as he also knew that if he was wrong about his attacker it would be a fatal try.

Discretion over valor, he reminded himself, especially when the odds were stacked against valor.

He had to get the rifleman into the open, he knew as he rubbed his hand across the flat leather holster around his calf with the double-edged throwing knife inside it. He'd coax the rifleman out, turn the tables. This time the cat would come into the open to be pounced upon. His glance went up to the trees and he chose a bur oak with thick, spreading branches, reached both arms up and closed his hands around the lowest branch. He pulled himself from the ground, lifted his body enough to get one leg over the branch and halted, hanging there for a long moment. He had moved with careful slowness so that not a single leaf had been disturbed, and now he waited, listening.

He heard nothing and he straightened to a sitting position on the branch, inched his way to a more solid spot near the trunk of the tree. He could see the ground below on both sides of the stream, and he stretched his body along the branch to lie there not unlike a strange serpent, coiled and waiting. The minutes grew longer and the silence heavier, and a cold smile came to Fargo's mouth. He was all but certain his attacker was neither a trailsman nor a Shoshoni hunter but an amateur in the ways of the hunt, unaware that waiting was the most important part of acting. Fargo guessed another ten minutes would bring the shooter to the end of his patience, and he lay relaxed on the branch. His smile twitched in satisfaction as he caught the movement below. Ten minutes, give or take a few long moments, and his hand moved to the holster around his leg.

His gaze on the ground below, he saw the figure step

cautiously around the trunk of the bur oak, bent in a half-crouch. Fargo's eyebrows rose as he looked down on the shock of medium brown hair with a soft curl to it. He saw a slender shape, a tan shirt pushing modestly outward and hanging loose over the tops of gray Levi's. *I'll be damned,* he swore silently, and drew his hand back from the calf holster. The girl crouched on one knee as she peered into the brush, a Kentucky Hawkens rifle with the shorter barrel held in her hands. She waited, continuing to peer into the brush, and he knew exactly what she was wondering. She wrestled with the thought that one of her shots had hit home and she took another cautious step forward.

He stared down at her, still recovering from his surprise. She brought still another new twist to everything, and he discarded his original plan to send the throwing knife through his attacker. But he had to remain careful. She was bent on putting lead through him. She'd demonstrated that all too clearly. He inched forward along the branch as she paused again, her head cocked to pick up any sound in the brush. She moved again. She'd be passing almost directly under him in seconds. He uncurled his legs from around the branch, half-rose, let another ten seconds go by, and leaped out of the tree. He'd timed his jump to come down on her with a grazing blow, and she pitched forward as he hit against her back and shoulders. She gave a short cry of surprise and the rifle went off as she hit the ground face forward. He had landed on his feet. He took a bouncing step and went after the rifle, which had fallen from her grasp.

He was just closing his hand around it when she whirled onto her side and kicked out at his wrist. He grunted in pain and the rifle fell from his grip. She was whirling, diving for it, when he caught her around the waist and flung her into the air. "Damn!" she swore as she hit the ground hard, taking a moment to shake her head and come up. But he had the rifle in his hands. He emptied the chamber and tossed the weapon aside as she flew at him. He ducked her furiously flailing blows, caught her around the knees, and dumped her in a half-somersault. Again she hit the ground hard and he heard her gasp of anger. But he had taken three long-legged strides and scooped the Colt up from beside the stream, and it was in his hand as he faced her. She had seized the rifle by the stock to use as a club, but she halted as she saw the revolver barrel aimed at her.

"That's better," Fargo said, really looking at her for the first time. He saw a face a little on the thin side yet pretty enough, the eyes a dark blue set wide apart, a small nose, nicely molded lips and a pert chin, the small features well balanced. A slender figure with what appeared to be modest breasts fitted the face, a small-boned body, also on the thin side, which avoided being scrawny by its compact firmness.

"Damn you, damn you," she breathed, pent-up fury in the words, and she took a step forward as she raised the rifle.

"Easy, now. Don't get stupid," Fargo warned.

"Then you better shoot, damn it. Go ahead, shoot me! What's one more to you?" she said and rushed at him, swinging the rifle. He easily avoided the blow, stuck his leg out, and she went sprawling, breasts bouncing under the loose shirt. But she was up instantly, still clutching the rifle as a club.

"What the hell are you talking about, girl?" Fargo asked.

"Maybe I know something, too. Go on and shoot," she said, running roughshod over his question.

"I don't know who you are or what you're talking about, honey, but I think you've been following the wrong trail," Fargo told her.

"Hell I have. You're the one who got Evie killed," she flung back, and Fargo's eyebrows lifted in surprise.

"Who the hell are you?" he growled.

"Glory Daley. Evie was my sister," the girl snapped. Fargo suddenly could see the resemblance—the thin face, the small features—but this young woman had none of Evie's wan, waiflike quality.

"You got her killed and you'll pay for it, damn you," Glory Daley said.

"Now, you back off, girl," Fargo said sternly. "I didn't get Evie killed. I was the one they were after. Evie just happened to be in their way."

Glory Daley sneered and her voice dripped with scorn. "Oh, sure, that's what you want everyone to think. Very clever. Only I know better."

"What do you know?" Fargo snapped at her.

"They came to kill Evie and you arranged to have her there so's they could do it," the young woman said, and Fargo caught the catch in her voice.

"You've got it all wrong. I didn't do anything of the kind," Fargo told her.

"I don't expect you'd say different," she returned. "But I know the truth. Those damn killers were after Evie. It was supposed to look like an attack on you, only it wasn't."

"Damn it, I didn't set it up," Fargo said. "Evie called me there to talk to me."

"Hand that to somebody else," Glory Daley said. "So

42

you can go ahead and shoot, because I won't stop till you pay for it.''

Fury, defiance, and pain—they were all in her small face. She believed in her accusation with the rage of the wounded. He couldn't reach her, couldn't penetrate the grief-stricken certainties she had drawn around herself, not with denials that were only words. He had to shock her, throw a curve that would make her at least listen to him. He grimaced inwardly. She simmered with rage, perhaps too much for anything to turn off. It would be a damn risk, he knew, but he decided to go for it. ''I'll prove you're wrong,'' he said.

She uttered a snort of scorn. ''Nothing you can say is going to do that, mister.''

''How about something I do?'' he thrust at her, and saw a tiny furrow come to her brow. He lowered the Colt, turned it in his hand, and held the gun out to her, butt-first. ''Go on, take it,'' he said. She peered warily at him, the furrow now a full frown. She carefully reached a hand out, her slender body tensed, ready to leap backward instantly. He stayed unmoving and she closed a hand around the butt of the Colt, yanked back, and raised the gun at once.

''What are you trying, mister?'' she asked suspiciously.

''I'm trying to get you to listen to me, damn it,'' he said. ''I just gave you my gun. Would I do that if I were lying to you?'' She continued to frown at him, but he saw her turning the question over in her mind. ''You know damn well I wouldn't,'' he said. She glowered back, but her silence was a kind of admission.

''What do you want to say?'' she muttered after another long moment.

''How about putting the gun down and we'll talk? You'll

still have it and I'll keep my distance. I just don't like taking chances," he said. She continued to frown but slowly lowered her hand to her side. "Thanks," he said. "First, the name's Fargo, Skye Fargo."

"I know. I heard around town," she said.

"Evie asked me to see her there. Duncan Kale had his men waiting, too. Evie was an innocent bystander," Fargo said.

"Evie was the target. Five bullets hit her. Not a one hit you. They weren't after you," Glory Daley spit out, and Fargo felt her words stab into him. The terrible moment flashed back through his thoughts. The attackers had loosed a hail of shots, but even when he rose and pulled Evie into the wall space their bullets thudded only into her. Had they really missed him? Fargo grimaced inwardly. He'd never considered it as anything but that, but now suddenly his head was pounding. He stared at Glory Daley. "Evie, not you," she said with quiet fierceness.

"You're so sure about that. You so sure about anything else?" he questioned.

"Such as?"

"Who? Why?"

"Somebody afraid of what Evie knew and might tell you," she said.

"Such as where Kale went, and Burt Dimmons with him?" Fargo asked, and Glory shrugged. "That brings it back to Kale. If that's so, why wouldn't he have his boys go after me, too? It doesn't make sense not to," Fargo pointed out.

"I don't know about making sense," Glory said. "But Evie was the target. I'm sure of that."

Fargo swore silently. He wanted to scoff again and

realized he couldn't. He could neither accept nor reject her certainty. "It doesn't add up," he said.

"Maybe it doesn't. Maybe they weren't from Kale. Maybe somebody else, then, but somebody afraid of what Evie might have known," she countered.

Her words hung in his mind. Somebody else with their own reasons for wanting Evie silenced. It wasn't beyond possibility. Maybe little Evie had known a lot about a lot of things. Nugget's remarks came to his thoughts, about all those in town who hated Petersen. "What can you tell me about Burt Dimmons?" he asked Glory.

"He was one of Petersen's strong-arm men and he loved Evie. That's all I know about him."

"Then it's safe to say a lot of people didn't love him."

"I guess not," Glory conceded.

"Evie wanted to protect him. Anybody who suspected that could've gone after her to stop her from doing that," Fargo pointed out, and Glory's little half-shrug was an admission. "Which means that there's only one fact here, girl. I didn't have anything to do with it. I didn't set Evie up, if she was who they were after," he finished.

She shrugged again and reached her arm out to him. "Take your gun," she said, a terrible weariness in her voice. His fingers closed around the Colt and he dropped the gun into its holster and stepped to her side. Her dark blue eyes held pain and fatigue as they met his. "Maybe I should say I'm sorry I almost killed you," she murmured. "I don't know."

"I'll consider it said," he told her. They walked together back to the Ovaro. "Where's your horse?" he asked.

"Down in the thick tree cover," she said, and strode away, her body swaying gracefully, her walk long-legged strength, a flat, tight little rear under the gray Levi's. She was astride a gray gelding when she returned, and he handed the rifle back to her.

"What now?" he asked.

"Back to my place till later," she said.

"Mind if I ride along?" he asked, and she shrugged agreement. "What do you do in Deerpole?" he asked as he rode beside her down the gentle slope.

"Pa left me a small trading post a half-mile west of town. I buy, sell, and trade off some items with the town stores."

"Evie wasn't part of it?" he queried.

"Evie was never part of anything. She and Pa never got along. He always thought she was weak, and because he thought so it made her more of an outsider," Glory said. "She drifted away from him, and after he died, from me. I tried to keep a hand out for her, but she never took it."

"What about her going to work at the dance hall?" he asked.

"She didn't have to do that. I'd have taken her in. She thought it was a safe place where Burt could find her if he came back," Glory said. "But she didn't expect he'd come back, not really. Some of the girls knew her and I think she went there as a place to gather herself for her next move. But in our own way, we were very close, Evie and I." Glory fell silent and Fargo stayed with her as they reached the bottom of the hills, where she bypassed Deerpole and finally drew up before a small, neat trading post, mostly log with a frame structure attached to the rear. He waited as she put the horse into a one-horse barn a few yards away.

"Been thinking about everything you said," Fargo told her when she returned. "I still say they were Kale's men and they were after me.'' Her mouth tightened in instant scorn. ''All the shots hit Evie, but stranger things than that have happened. There's no point in chasing off in all directions.''

''You're going after Duncan Kale for the Petersens,'' Glory said, and he nodded. ''I'm going to get whoever sent those killers,'' she said.

''I'll find Kale. I'm thinking that'll be one and the same thing and he'll pay for Evie,'' Fargo said. ''That's a promise.''

Her dark blue eyes searched his face for another moment. ''Thanks. I guess I had you figured all wrong in this,'' she said.

''You guess?''

''All right, I had it wrong,'' she conceded. ''You going to the burial?''

''I plan to.''

''Maybe we can talk later,'' she said, a cryptic edge to the remark as she turned and went into the small trading store. Fargo sent the Ovaro off in a slow trot, headed for Deerpole. The day had already passed noon and the sun had begun to slide westward. He halted before Nugget's shack, dismounted, and started to enter just as the white-haired figure appeared in the doorway. No bottle in his hand, Fargo noted, and the old miner's eyes were clear.

''What brings you back?'' Nugget asked with a trace of belligerance. ''You said your piece before.''

''That was about staying sober. This is about Glory Daley,'' Fargo said.

Nugget uttered a snort. ''Met her, did you?''

''She damn near blew my head off,'' Fargo said, and quickly told the old miner about his introduction to Glory and of the accusations she had made with such certainty.

When he'd finished, Nugget stared into space for a full minute.

"Got anything that says she might be right?" Fargo questioned.

"No, I don't," Nugget said. "No names, no talk, if that's what you mean."

"What do you think?"

"As you said, Fargo, logic points to Kale and strange things happen, but I can't say she couldn't be right, either," the old miner said.

Fargo gave a wry grunt as he mounted his horse. Nugget had reinforced his own conclusions. But he'd also kept alive the nagging question. A shower of bullets that had struck only Evie. A strange happenstance? Coincidence? One of those things that just happen? Or something more? He knew the wondering would stay inside him. Reason and logic were sometimes such pale allies.

3

Clouds had come to hide the late afternoon sun. Appropriate, Fargo thought as he sat atop the Ovaro under the grayness at the foot of the burial hill. Dolly and her girls had come. The sheriff, too. Nugget leaned against a headstone to one side. Glory, in a black shirt and black skirt, was a slender figure standing alone to his left. They made up the total of the mourners. The minister, also the town barber, Fargo had learned, mercifully confined his words to scripture, and it was done with in a few minutes. Fargo stayed atop the Ovaro to one side as the others drifted away, and he saw Glory coming toward him.

"Can we talk some more? At my place?" she asked. Her face was somber but composed.

"Tonight," he said. She gave an almost imperceptible nod and walked on. He turned to look for Nugget, but found the old miner had already disappeared. He spurred the pinto into a walk that became a trot only when he reached the road leading from town. He crossed the low hills as the grayness darkened, the day sliding toward its end. Finally he found the dish-shaped dip of land with the ranch in its center. Joanna Petersen stepped from the house as he reined to a halt and swung from the horse. She wore a full-length dark blue lounging gown with a deep V at the neck, her almost blond hair again pulled back by the bone clip.

"I expected you earlier," she said with a hint of reproach.

"Got delayed," he answered, and instantly wondered why he hadn't told her he'd waited for Evie's funeral. She probably had guessed as much, he told himself, but was dissatisfied with the answer. He'd wanted to distance himself from the incident, he admitted silently, and felt slightly ashamed of it. He followed Joanna as she went into the house and he saw the servant wheeling the wheelchair and its occupant away from the table. J. B. Petersen's gaunt face seemed a death mask and the watery blue eyes stared at nothing.

Joanna passed her father without a pause, without a moment's touch, not even a glance or gesture. Fargo found himself surprised by the seeming coldness, and his eyes narrowed on her as she turned to face him inside the big living room. But she was sharp and perceptive and read the disapproval in his eyes before he'd had a chance to mask it, he realized. "I can't stand to see him this way. I have to shut myself off to live with it and function," Joanna said.

Fargo winced inside for unjust assumptions. "It must be hard," he said, apology in his voice.

"You have things to ask me," she said, and folded herself onto the leather sofa, the deep neckline of the dress letting the top of one full breast spill into view. As he slid down beside her his nostrils drew in the faint scent of gardenia.

"Where did a good-looking woman like you fit into your pa's business plans?" Fargo asked. "Kale was his partner."

"I supervised the household, saw to Daddy's appointments, played hostess when he entertained, and generally looked charming," she said.

"I imagine you did that very well."

"Compliments? How unexpected," Joanna murmured, her lips curving into a smile.

"I'm full of surprises," Fargo said. "Describe Duncan Kale for me."

"Tall and handsome, wears long sideburns, straight black hair, very blue eyes, and a thin mustache," Joanna told him.

"Burt Dimmons?"

"Medium height, oxlike build, a heavy face and a receding hairline. He has a small scar on his upper lip."

"You said you had leads," Fargo reminded her.

"Maybe not exactly leads, but I know what Duncan always dreamed of doing. He used to talk to me about it. He always wanted to be a gold miner. Not the grubby kind who sift through mud in sluices all day. That wasn't for him. Duncan wanted to have enough money to buy a mine and build it up and expand. He wanted to hire others to do the mine work, the way the Murphy boys, Sutter and Comstock did, until he became a big mine operator."

"So you think he's taken off for gold-mining country," Fargo said, and she nodded.

"Not anywhere, though. He wouldn't go down into

Arizona or southern California. He hates the heat," she said.

"That only leaves west, north, or east across the Bighorn Mountains," Fargo said, and she heard the unsaid in the remark and gave a small shrug.

"All right, it's not much of a help," she murmured.

"The gold-mine part may be, later," Fargo said. "Burt Dimmons left with him. Was he in on the embezzlement?"

She reflected for a moment. "I'm not sure how much Burt Dimmons knew, but he was Duncan's right-hand man." Fargo thought of how Nugget had described him as Duncan Kale's strong-arm man. Maybe Dimmons had other reasons to flee with his boss.

"Any more of your men go with them?" Fargo queried.

"No."

"He take any wagons?"

"No, but he took three extra horses," she said.

Fargo's lips pursed. "That means something," he said. Joanna looked at him questioningly. "Extra horses usually mean hard high-mountain riding that quickly tires horses. He took all his personal things, too, I imagine."

"Yes," she said.

"That means he probably had a pack horse, too. Two riders, three extra horses, and one pack horse. That gives me something I can use," Fargo said. "And makes me even more certain they planned on hard mountain riding." He stood up and Joanna rose with him. "I'm going to scout around for a day or two. It might save me going a lot of wrong trails," he said.

"You're the expert," she answered. "But make sure you stop back here before you set out after them."

"You're the boss," he said. She reached into a pocket

at the side of the gown, drew out a roll of bills, and pushed them into his hand.

"Payment as agreed upon, from the J. B. Petersens," she said, took a quick step closer, and suddenly her lips were on his for a softly moist instant. "Special thanks from this J. B. Petersen," she murmured.

"How unexpected," he said, the echo in his smile.

"I'm full of surprises," she returned deftly and stepped back.

"I'll remember that," he said as she watched him walk to the Ovaro from the doorway. He rode away with a wave that drew no answer, but he felt her eyes on him as he disappeared into the night. A most interesting woman, Joanna Petersen, he reflected, and wondered if the poised control ever really left her. He turned the horse east across a low hill and stayed at a fast trot until he reached the little trading post, where a light still burned inside.

Glory answered his knock, clad in Levi's and a dark green shirt hanging out over her jeans, her dark blue eyes sharp, speculation in her glance as she led him into a simply furnished room. He took in a fabric-covered sofa along one wall, a thick Indian beaded rug on the floor, chairs and a small fireplace and an open-faced cabinet. "When are you going?" she asked.

"Day, maybe two. I want to scout some myself first, in the general area," he said.

"I still think they were after Evie, not you, but if it was Kale, I want to make sure he pays," Glory said. "Nugget and I talked about it. We want to go along with you."

"Forget it," he said. "I work alone."

"We could help," she said.

"Sure. A suspicious spitfire and an old drunk. No, thanks," Fargo said.

"Nugget will stay sober. He said this is the first real reason he's had to do so in twenty years," Glory said.

"No dice, honey."

"Joanna Petersen's paying you, but Evie was my sister. I've a right," Glory said.

"Go track him down yourself."

"Hear me out. You owe me that much," Glory said, and he lowered himself onto the sofa. She gracefully folded herself across from him, legs tucked under her. "First, you may need help. You don't know what you may run into. Second, you don't know what Kale or Burt Dimmons looks like. I can point them out to you."

"Joanna gave me descriptions," Fargo said.

"Not enough. Kale could shave his mustache off, same with his sideburns, and cut his hair short. He'd look different. You wouldn't recognize him, but Nugget and I would," she said. "Because we've seen him. More important, if he knows the Petersens sent for you he could have his own men waiting and watching. They'd be looking for a single rider, not two men and a woman who seem to be prospecting. Luckily, neither Kale nor Dimmons knows Nugget or me."

Fargo frowned into space. There was sense in her words. Some kind of disguise might help in getting into a gold-mining operation, he pondered, brought in a few thoughts of his own, and finally returned his gaze to Glory. "One condition only," he said. "You do what I ask, when I ask, whatever it turns out to be."

It was her turn to frown. "I don't like buying a pig in a poke."

"And I don't like debates after I make a decision. That's the deal. Take it or leave it," he said sharply.

She thought a moment longer. "All right, it's a deal," she said, and he rose. She unfolded herself with quick lithe grace. "There's an extra room. You can stay the night."

"I want to be in the hills come dawn. But thanks," he said, and turned away as he walked from the house, leaving behind a small figure that drew strength from her own inner anger. He saw the light go out as he rode away and he was in the hills before he reined to a halt beneath red fir, unsaddled the Ovaro, and lay down on his bedroll and let plans form in his mind.

The Big Belt Mountains lay directly to the west, and further west just beyond them the full ruggedness of the Cabinet Mountains. To the north, the Lewis Range—but that was too far north. Southwest lay the Sapphire Mountains, and east was mostly non-mountainous country. He tried to put himself into the shoes of a man he'd never met and knew damn little about and realized that knowing little about Duncan Kale might be an advantage. His mind had to stay uncluttered with only the very basics to work with, and they remained the same. The man had fled but not in haste. He'd taken a pack horse and three extra horses. That wasn't a man who felt the need to ride hard and light. That was a man who didn't expect immediate pursuit. But he'd prepared for mountain riding, and Fargo decided that the most traveled road alongside the Big Belt Mountains would be his first goal. His decision made, he let sleep sweep over him.

He was in the saddle with the early sun, quickly finding the road that led northwest, and by late morning he found a traveler's way station with an attached stable. A beefy-faced man in overalls thought hard at his question. "Two months ago? Too far back for my remembering," he said. At Fargo's insistence he told of two other traveler's inns, one on a road that headed north, the other at the beginning of a passage directly west. Fargo chose the closer one first and it was late afternoon when he reached his goal, a well-tended log structure run by a husband and wife. They received a lot of wagon trade, he saw by the marks on the ground. Neither had any recollection of their guests two months back. "So many pass through, stay only a night. We can't remember," the woman said, and Fargo moved on his way.

Night descended and he slept under a thick-branched box elder. In the morning, he rode along a narrow passage that finally brought him to another traveler's inn, this time a small house with six cabins surrounding it. Two brothers ran the place, their families helping out, he learned. "About two months ago," one brother reflected. "Yes, I think I remember them," he said, and Fargo felt his pulse rate go up. "We weren't busy at that time. In fact, they were our only customers, that's why I remember them. Two men, three extra horses, and a pack horse."

"They tell you which way they were heading when they left?" Fargo questioned.

"They didn't tell me, but I heard them talking about passing north of Missoula," the man said.

"That'll do me," Fargo said, and turned the pinto back the way he had come. They had headed northwest. They'd probably stopped at Missoula Snow Bow. There were saloons and stopping places this side of the Cabinet Mountains. He'd go from one to the next, not unlike a frog leaping from lily pad to lily pad. There was one more thing in his favor. Wherever Kale had finally settled down, he'd obviously decided to protect himself with a channel into Deerpole. He probably had others on the watch, as Glory had anticipated, and Fargo was glad for that. A channel was a two-way passage and those who waited to kill could be killed, and each one would point the way. It'd be a deadly game, but it was probably the one thing that made it not complete needle-in-a-haystack foolishness. It'd be the thing that turned a near-impossible two-month-old cold trail into a flickering beacon.

The day turned to night and he rode on. The moon was high in the blue-velvet sky when he reached Glory Daley's trading post. The house was still and dark and he thought of turning away, but he was damn tired and grimness churned inside him. He knocked and it took a few minutes before she answered, cotton nightgown on her slender body, a five-shot, dull-gray Remington-Beals pocket revolver in her hand. "I'll take that extra room," he said.

"Of course," she said, quickly wiping the surprise from her face. She waited while he unsaddled the horse and took his saddlebag with him. She led the way, her nightgown falling straight from the tips of her breasts, and showed him into a small room with a cot against one wall. Moonlight coming in through a lone window outlined a small dresser. "Will you need a lamp?" she asked.

"No, just sleep," he said, and she closed the door behind her without another word. He undressed, fell across the cot, and was asleep in seconds, waking only when the first warm yellow light of the new sun probed its way through the window. He indulged himself with another half-hour of relaxation and finally rose, found a washbasin with water in it and washed. When he finished dressing he walked from the room to find Glory beside a bubbling coffee pot, dark brown hair freshly combed, a white shirt tucked in at the waist and tight against her small breasts. Levi's enclosed her slender legs.

She poured coffee into a china mug and produced hot rolls and bacon. He sat across from her at a small table. "Found a jumping-off place," he said.

"I'll get Nugget and have him meet me here," Glory said.

"Both of you meet me at the Petersen place mid-afternoon," Fargo said.

"Not until then?" Glory frowned in surprise.

"My horse needs a good rubdown and I want his left foreshoe checked," Fargo said. "Mid-afternoon. Thanks for the room and for breakfast."

"Some of us are rich and can pay, some of us can't do more than simple things, breakfast and a room for the night," she said, just a hint of defensiveness in her voice.

"Nothing wrong with simple things," Fargo said.

She walked outside with him and watched while he saddled the Ovaro. He saw the jumble of thoughts mirrored in her eyes before he rode away and she returned to the house. He rode fast, turned east to stop at the Petersen place before he went to town. J. B. Petersen was outside in his wheelchair, sitting in the sun with the servant nearby. He stared straight ahead with eyes that seemed unseeing, his figure rigid in the chair, and Fargo found himself staring at the man.

"What are you thinking?"

The voice broke into his thoughts and he turned to see that Joanna had come from the stable, her gray-blue eyes holding a private amusement.

"Wondering, mostly," Fargo said.

"About what?"

"About what life can do to us. About how quickly a man can go from being powerful to being pitied," Fargo said.

"I don't think back anymore," she said. "What did you find out?" Again he felt the apparent coldness in her answer, but he had misjudged that once and he wasn't about to do it again.

"Found a place to start," he said.

"You leaving right away?" She frowned, concern suddenly in her voice.

"Mid-afternoon. I'll stop by before I go," he said.

"Good." She nodded and he rode from the ranch. As he left, he saw Joanna hurry back to the stable. He rode on into town, where he was lucky to find the smithy able to tend to his horse after only an hour's wait. The left forefoot needed a new shoe. After that was done, Fargo stopped at the J. B. Petersen Feed Store for an extra bag of oats. A horse needed extra oats for hard mountain riding. It was nearing mid-afternoon when he finally rode onto the Petersen land again, and he immediately noticed some ten horses tethered to one side, their riders lounging nearby. Joanna came from the stable, clad in riding britches with a white shirt that clung tight around her deep breasts, the almost blond hair held back again. She had a good-looking bay in tow and she halted before him.

"I'm ready," she said.

"For what?" He frowned.

"For going with you."

"Hell you are."

"But I am. And I'm taking those men."

"Shove it, honey," he said. "I won't find him leading a damn expedition."

"Look, I want Duncan Kale alive if possible. I want

a chance to get back everything he stole. Or, if he's killed, I want to be there to go through his things and find whatever I can," Joanna said. "I have to be there."

"With all those gunslingers?"

"They might be needed."

"I'm telling you, I won't find Kale with a posse riding herd," Fargo said.

"All right, we'll start out with them. I'll have them drop back as soon as you tell me it's time for that. It'll be your decision. That's fair enough, isn't it?" Joanna said. "I just want them where I can call on them if we need to."

Fargo grimaced. Her offer failed to make him happy. He was still turning it over in his mind when Glory and Nugget appeared and rode to a halt. Nugget, atop a gray mare, had a saddlepack with a shovel and pickax sticking out from it. Glory rode a good, sturdy roan mare and Fargo watched Joanna fasten the two new arrivals with a cool stare that finally turned to him. "What's this?"

"It is Evie's sister," Fargo said.

"I know who it is," Joanna said. "And everyone knows the town drunk. What are they doing here?"

"Coming with me," Fargo said.

"She's coming with you?" Joanna frowned, and he nodded. "No wonder you didn't want anyone else along. You're bringing your own party entertainment."

"Watch your tongue, sister," Glory cut in. "Being a Petersen doesn't impress me any."

"I'm taking Glory because I think she might be helpful," Fargo said.

Joanna's eyes went to Nugget. "Next you'll be telling me he's the chaperone."

"That might just be the right word." Fargo smiled. "In

any case, it's my decision. You live with it or kiss me good-bye.''

Joanna's eyes narrowed. "I don't have much choice, do I?" she tossed back.

"Look, you hired me because I know what I'm doing. Let me do it my way," he said, summoning reasonableness.

"And my men?" she asked.

Fargo grunted inwardly. The men wouldn't be a problem at the start. He'd compromise with her for now. "All right, until I say differently. I'm taking you up on that," he answered, and she nodded agreement and climbed onto her horse. "A damn parade," he muttered as he swung onto the Ovaro and led the way northward. Joanna came up to ride beside him. Glory and Nugget rode together a half-dozen strides behind, and Joanna's posse stayed together at the rear. He was glad to see that Joanna had the good sense not to make conversation, and they reached the beginning of the road he had taken to the second traveler's inn with the six cabins as night fell. He found a cleared place off the road to camp and Joanna tethered her bay next to the Ovaro.

"Where are we heading?" she asked.

"A traveler's inn and then west from there. Two men and three horses stayed there and went west, probably to Snow Bow, south of Missoula," he told her. "From there they probably kept west by northwest. There are major goldfields out of Bannack and Couer d'Alene in the Oregon Territory. We'll see what we find."

"I'm going to visit the men. I'd like you to come along," she said. He shrugged, finished unsaddling his horse, and went with her to where the small posse had bedded down in a semicircle. The men rose as she reached them and one stepped forward, a small, wiry figure with a sharp face. "This is Gus Harby, Fargo," she introduced. "Gus is sort of foreman, you might say. I've explained to everyone that you'll be giving the orders."

Fargo's smile was a mask. She had hired them and they would look to her as the one who gave the final orders. She knew it. Her words were simply appeasement tossed out to him like an old bone. Joanna underestimated him, he reflected. "That's nice," he said, and his eyes moved across the men. They were a nondescript lot, hired guns, not gunfighters.

"Anything you want us to know, Fargo?" Gus Harby asked, but Fargo caught his quick glance at Joanna.

"For now, when we reach a town, you boys stay on your own. You're not with us," Fargo said.

"I got it," Harby said, and after a few more unimportant words with the men, Joanna strolled away and Fargo walked beside her.

"Feel better now?" she asked.

"Much," Fargo said.

She paused for a moment as she took her bedroll from her horse. "I'm sorry I was so abrupt earlier when Glory Daley appeared. I shouldn't have jumped to conclusions," she said.

"Usually a mistake," he said blandly.

"Maybe there was more to it than that."

"Such as?" he asked, his brows raised.

"I'm not sure yet," she said. "Good night." She took her bedroll and disappeared behind a tree and he walked on with his own gear to pause where Glory was sitting up, partly covered by her blanket, a grayish-white cotton nightgown tied high at the neck. Nugget had bedded down near her, Fargo noted.

"You and Joanna work things out?" Glory asked, a hint of waspishness in her tone.

"For the moment," he said.

"She had her nerve saying those things."

"People say wrong things when they're taken by surprise," he offered.

"No surprise. She wanted you all to herself."

"You're reaching, honey," Fargo said.

"Maybe not that way, though I'm not sure about that," Glory said. "But she wants to make sure you do what she wants when she wants. She's that type. You can tell her I won't get in her way."

"I'll do that," Fargo said, and walked on into the darkness. He'd gone perhaps a dozen strides when her voice followed.

" 'Less I change my mind," she called, and he smiled as he kept walking. He found a hillock with high brush and set his bedroll out. He undressed, laid his gun alongside the bedroll, and stretched out as Glory's words hung inside him. They had been close enough to truth in one respect. Joanna Petersen was used to getting her own way. Wealth and position had been her weapons for that. But Glory liked having her own way, too. Fierce independence and pride had been her weapons. Now both thirsted for vengeance, yet the character of their vengeance was very different. Joanna's rose from righteous fury at having been deceived and robbed. Glory's rose out of pain. Two women, so alike in a few things, so different in everything else.

Maybe he'd never find Duncan Kale, Fargo mused. But

the search might prove more interesting than he'd expected. He closed his eyes and slept until he woke with the first towhee's call in the morning. He rose, trudged down to the Ovaro wearing only trousers and gunbelt, and used his canteen to wash. When he finished, he saw Glory sitting up watching him, her eyes taking in the muscled symmetry of his torso. She turned away quickly when she saw him watching her, and he smiled as he finished dressing.

A stand of wild plums furnished breakfast for everybody. They reached the traveler's inn by noon, stayed to have lunch and rest the horses before Fargo led the way west. The land quickly grew mountainous, and making time was put aside as the horses pulled up fairly steep passes. When Fargo halted at a mountain stream to water the horses, Joanna sat down beside him, Glory and Nugget only a few feet away. "Where are we going?" she asked.

"Missoula Snow Bow. I figure we'll reach it by late tomorrow," Fargo said. "It's a good bet that Kale stopped there."

"Why?"

"He'd want one good night's rest at least before going into the Bitterroot Range. It's also a good bet that if he left lookouts they'll be there," Fargo said.

"Why?" Joanna asked again.

"He'd know that anyone following would likely stop there," Fargo said.

"If he left lookouts they'll be expecting a lone rider. We know he knows I sent for you. You'll want us to stay with you so they won't spot you," Joanna said.

"No. You all bed down outside town. I'll go in alone," Fargo said.

"That doesn't make sense. One of the reasons we came is to help you move without being spotted," Glory cut in.

"That's right. When the time comes. This isn't the time for that," Fargo said.

Glory frowned at him. "You're going to set yourself up as a target to see if he has anyone waiting for you," she said.

"Give that girl a cigar," Fargo said.

"I can't permit that," Joanna interjected with cold austerity. "I didn't hire you to make yourself a target and possibly get killed. I hired you to find Duncan Kale. That comes first."

"I figure this is one part of it," Fargo said.

"No. That's absolutely too risky," Joanna said.

Fargo gave her a cool glance. "Aren't you forgetting something, honey? I call the shots, remember?" he said.

"I didn't expect you to jeopardize everything by this sort of fool behavior," Joanna snapped back. "You're making yourself bait."

"Where do you find bait, honey?" Fargo asked, his voice hardening.

Joanna paused for a moment before answering. "In a trap," she said finally.

Fargo smiled. "Mount up," he said, and pushed to his feet. He paused as he passed Glory and met her skeptical glance.

"Traps can backfire," she muttered, and strode past him. He climbed onto the Ovaro and led the way west again. They kept moving through low passageways until Fargo pulled off to camp as the day drew to an end. He finished eating a dried beef strip, saw Joanna bedding down nearby, Glory and Nugget a short distance away, and the men off by themselves. He took his bedroll and made his way through the blackness of the trees, climbed a gentle slope, and settled down under the four-sided branchlets of a Rocky Mountain juniper. He undressed to his drawers, the Colt at his side once again, and stretched out in the warm night. He had almost drifted off to sleep when he heard the sound of footsteps moving through the trees, hesitant, uncertain steps. He sat up on one elbow, his hand closing over the Colt, and strained his eyes, finally picked up the shadowed shape.

"Looking for someone?" he asked, his voice soft yet carrying through the darkness, the Colt positioned and ready to fire. He saw the dark shape change direction and move toward him, take on form as it neared and become Joanna wrapped in a dark robe. He put the Colt down and she came to the edge of the bedroll and lowered herself to the ground.

"Insomnia?" he asked.

"Came to talk to you," she said. "About earlier today. I know it sounded wrong. I just don't want to see anything happen to you."

"That makes two of us," he said blandly.

"I need you, Fargo. You have to understand."

"I guess I do."

"You have to be careful."

"I believe in that." He smiled.

Joanna leaned forward and her arms lifted, slid around his neck. Her mouth pressed his, full lips extremely soft. The robe parted and the tops of her deep breasts rose up over the edge of the nightgown she wore. Her mouth clung and pulled back only when his hand moved to touch the skin at the top of one breast. "For understanding," she murmured.

66

"I can be more understanding," he remarked.

"Yes, I'm sure you can," she said.

"Maybe you need me in more ways than you know," he said, and watched her lips purse as she stood up and pulled her robe closed.

"Maybe," she said thoughtfully. "Maybe." She let her gaze move slowly across the muscled smoothness of his body. "All the more reason for you to be careful," she said, then turned and hurried away. He watched her figure melt into the night, lay back and drew sleep around himself.

4

When the morning sun cast its yellow net over the land, Fargo rose, dressed, and returned to where the others had just begun to wake. Except for Glory. She was dressed and saddling the roan mare. He caught the glance she tossed his way and he halted. "You've an edge in your eye this morning," he said.

"No edge. Just curiosity," she said.

"Bull," he grunted.

"You enjoy your night?" she slid at him as she adjusted the stirrup leather.

"Spying one of your talents?" he returned.

"No spying. I didn't sleep well last night," she said.

"And you saw Joanna leave the camp," he finished, and she nodded. "She wanted to explain about how things sounded. Sort of an apology, you could say," Fargo told her.

"Not me," Glory sniffed. "Things sounded just the way they were meant. She was just trying to mend fences."

"Aren't you being pretty harsh?"

"No. You find Duncan Kale and she won't give a damn about how you risk your neck afterwards."

"Hell, you agreed with her. You didn't want me to do it, either. I could think the same thing about you," Fargo said.

"You'd be wrong."

"Just like you're wrong about her."

"Only I'm not," Glory said stubbornly. "Anyway, you didn't answer my question. You enjoy the night?"

"If you'd stayed awake you'd have seen that she didn't visit for long," he told her. "Not that it's any of your damn business."

Her lips thinned as she glowered at him. "No, I suppose not," she said. "I just don't like to see anybody taken in."

"Sounds more like jealousy to me," Fargo said.

"Don't you wish!" she snapped, tightened the stirrup, and stalked away. Fargo's chuckle followed her. He began to saddle the Ovaro as the rest of the camp came awake. He found Nugget at his side as he finished, the old miner's wrinkled face wrinkling even more so as he grimaced.

"Couldn't help overhearing you and Glory," he said.

"You going to side with her?" Fargo asked.

"No, except that she's not the kind that imagines things. I want to ask you about one thing you said yesterday."

"About bait being found in a trap?" Fargo said, and Nugget nodded.

"You've something planned," the old miner said.

"That's right, and you've saved me the trouble of coming to you," Fargo said. "I'll still be the bait, but you're going to be part of the trap."

"Now you're talking, mister. You just tell me what, where, and when."

"Over here," Fargo said, stepping to the edge of the trees. "This is between us, nobody else, and that includes Glory."

"I understand," Nugget said, and listened intently as Fargo outlined his plans in short, terse sentences. Nugget nodded when he finished, his face grave, and Fargo left him to get his things ready. Joanna appeared, cool and commandingly attractive in a tailored tan shirt and tan riding britches. She swung in beside him as he led the way forward through the low passages. He kept a steady pace with only a few stops to rest, and the day was growing long when he led the way downward through a wide pass. The collection of buildings that was Missoula Snow Bow rose up at the end of a narrow plateau, and Fargo drew to a halt as dusk began to descend.

"You can bed down here," Fargo said, gesturing at a clearing in a stand of hackberry. He saw Joanna's instant frown.

"You going into town alone? You're going to go on with it?" she asked.

"That's right," Fargo said.

"I thought, after last night . . ." she began, and let the sentence trail off.

"That I'd changed my mind? You thought wrong," he said. Joanna's eyes held anger as she turned away, took her things, and flung them down under a gnarled and low-branched tree.

"You've upset the queen bee," Glory remarked as he passed near, waspishness in her voice.

"Some people get upset when they care," Fargo said.

"Some people get upset when they don't get their way," Glory said.

"It's plain you're not bothered any," Fargo said.

"I wasn't fool enough to think you'd changed your mind," Glory said smugly, and walked to where Nugget had set out their things. Fargo exchanged glances with the old miner as he went by.

The night descended quickly. Fargo relaxed against a thin hackberry and let the camp settle down to sleep. Only when it had grown silent did he get to his feet and walk the Ovaro from the clearing. When he was far enough away from the camp, he swung onto the horse and set out across the narrow plateau under a three-quarter moon. He slowed when he reached the buildings of the darkened town and found the saloon a little past the town's center.

He dropped the Ovaro's reins over the far end of the hitching rail and strolled to the saloon doors. The Snow Bow Saloon was just that and no more, he noted. No dance hall or pleasure palace attached as with so many saloons. All the better, he thought. Fewer distractions. For everyone. He strolled into the saloon, sweeping the room with a quick glance. He took in a bar along one wall, not crowded, some ten tables scattered around the rest of the room. It was a narrow place, the tables crowded together. He went to the bar and ordered a bourbon from a portly, gray-haired bartender. The man poured from a bottle labeled Bardstown Bourbon and Fargo nodded his head in appreciation affter the first sip.

His gaze moved across the tables again, more slowly this time. Four were taken by card players, a fifth by an old man mumbling to his own bottle of whiskey. At another table against the wall two men leaned back, and Fargo saw their eyes on him. He took another draw of the bourbon. There was a drink in front of each man, but neither had touched it, he noted. The saloon doors opened and two men entered and immediately walked to the bar. Fargo's glance flicked to the two figures against the wall and saw their eyes watching the two newcomers. The saloon doors opened again, this time for a tall, thin figure in black shirt and black jeans. The man sauntered to a table and sat down, and the two men against the wall watched him intently too.

Fargo's eyes narrowed for a moment as he took another pull of the bourbon. He waited till the bartender had served the man in black before he ordered another bourbon and saw the two men looking at another man who'd entered the saloon. They still hadn't touched their drinks, he noted, and caught their gaze moving over the room with slow deliberation. Fargo sipped his second bourbon. He wasn't ready yet. He wanted to make sure to allow enough time. Three of the bar patrons left and four new ones entered, and again he saw the two men examine each new arrival.

He waited, this time for their eyes to circle back to him, before he spoke to the bartender. "Slow night?" he asked.

"About average. We get more of a crowd on weekends," the bartender answered. "Traders and trappers come in then. We don't get much trade from folks moving through. Maybe because there aren't that many."

"Well, I'm one of them," Fargo said, keeping his voice casual but loud enough for anyone to hear. "I'm trailing somebody. He may have passed through here a few months back."

"A few months back? I'd call that a cold trail, mister," the bartender said.

"Name's Fargo, Skye Fargo. And the trail's heated up," Fargo said. "You by chance remember a man stopping by here, might have had another man with him, and three extra horses? He might've stayed in town a few days.

Duncan Kale, if he used his right name—tall, black hair, thin mustache.''

The bartender frowned as he searched his memory. "Can't say that I do," he muttered. Fargo smiled. He hadn't really expected the man to recall anything. He'd kept his attention fully on the bartender during the conversation and now he casually let his gaze move out across the room. The table against the wall was empty, the two glasses still there. Fargo smiled again. He'd struck paydirt. The bait had worked. They had left to set up their ambush. Or maybe to get help. Fargo held the thought. He had to be prepared for that. He toyed with the bourbon, waited another five minutes, then downed the last of the drink. Nugget had had more than enough time to arrive and no one had entered the saloon for the last ten minutes.

"Got another question," Fargo said to the bartender. "Those two gents that were sitting against the wall with the drinks they didn't touch. You know them?"

"Can't say I know them, but they've been coming in every night for a week. They each order a drink, don't touch it, and just sit back. They leave when I close up. Sometimes they toss down their drinks then. They don't talk to anybody or cause any trouble."

"They just wait." Fargo smiled once more.

The bartender nodded. "Seems that way."

"I don't think they'll be back," Fargo said casually, and drew a raised eyebrow from the bartender. "You have a rear door out of here?"

"Through that curtain," the man said, nodding at an arched doorway hung with a silk drape.

"Much obliged," Fargo said, and was through the drape in a half-dozen long strides. A storage room opened on the other side of the curtain and beyond that the rear door. Fargo opened the door with silent caution, paused, and slipped outside into the night. The three-quarter moon offered enough light for him to see and he turned the corner from the saloon and peered down a narrow alleyway. A figure crouched at the far end of the alley, gun in hand, looking out at the entrance to the saloon. Fargo drew the Colt as he moved, his footsteps silent as a mountain lion's padded prowl. The second man was also out there waiting, possibly across the street; they were hoping to catch their quarry in a cross fire.

The figure in the alley, all his concentration on the doorway of the saloon, never heard Fargo until he felt the barrel of the Colt press against his neck. "One wrong move and your head's gone," Fargo whispered, and felt the man grow stiff. "Drop the gun," he said, and heard the sound of the pistol as it hit the dirt. Fargo's left arm encircled the man's neck as he kept the Colt pressed against him. "Where's your friend?" Fargo questioned.

"He left."

Fargo pulled the hammer back on the Colt, the sound loud in the man's ear. "A wrong answer's the same as a wrong move," Fargo hissed. "One more time. Where is he?"

"Out there," the man said, fear in his voice.

"Where?"

"Across the street."

Fargo's gaze went to the building opposite the saloon, a flat-roofed storage depot. A row of boxes lined the front of the building. A gunman would be hunkered down behind them, protected from direct fire. Fargo's eyes narrowed. It was more or less what he had expected.

They'd had enough time to wait. They would have made plans. Now there was one last thing. He pressed the Colt harder into the man's neck. "He have company?" Fargo rasped.

"No," the man said, too quickly, too eagerly.

"You're lying," Fargo said. "Too bad." He jammed the Colt hard into the man's neck.

"All right, all right," the man croaked.

"How many?" Fargo growled.

"Two."

"Where?"

"With him."

Fargo's arm tightened around the man's neck. "Let's find out," he rasped, and pushed the man forward out of the alley. Keeping his body against the man's, he propelled the figure forward along the front of the saloon.

"No, Jesus, no," the man choked and then, raising his voice to a shout. "No, don't shoot! It's me . . . don't shoot!" His answer was two shots that came from behind the boxes. Fargo spun the man around as he stayed behind him and felt the shots thud into the man's body. "Aw, Jesus . . . Jesus," the man gasped. He began to go down, his legs sagging. Fargo went down with him, keeping his hold around the man's neck, and the next fusillade of shots split the night to slam into the man's body. Fargo saw the two figures, but they were on the roof of the building, firing down from the edge.

His back against the wall of the saloon, the body still in front of him, Fargo brought the Colt up and fired. One of the figures on the roof toppled forward and plummeted to the ground. The next shot that exploded the night was the deep, heavy sound of a rifle, and Fargo saw the figure fall sideways from behind the row of boxes and lie still.

Fargo got off another shot at the second man on the roof, but the figure was fleeing, disappearing from sight, and Fargo pushed to his feet from behind the lifeless figure. He saw Nugget rise, rifle in hand, from alongside the building next to the warehouse.

Nugget waved and came forward. "One of them's still out there," Fargo said, and the words had just left his lips when he heard the sound of a horse being sent into a gallop. The ambushers had left their horses at the rear of the building. Fargo swore as he whirled and raced for the Ovaro. "I'm going after him," he called to Nugget as he vaulted onto the pinto and sent the horse down the space alongside the warehouse and the next building. He could hear the fleeing dry-gulcher riding hard through the bank of trees.

He followed the sound as the Ovaro quickly gained ground, and on the other side of the trees he saw a small trail that sloped upward through a stand of junipers. He took it and listened to the rider ahead of him crashing through high brush. The man had left the trail and Fargo slowed as he reached the spot where the brush lay pushed aside to the right of the pass. He veered, followed through the brush. The rider ahead continued his headlong flight, probably unaware he was being pursued, Fargo decided. Suddenly the sound of the racing horse vanished. The man had pulled up and Fargo instantly reined the Ovaro to a halt. The man hadn't stopped more than a hundred yards on and Fargo swung to the ground and went forward on foot.

He pushed through the thick brush as silently as he could and yet make time, and suddenly he saw a shack rise up in a small cleared space, a lamp burning inside. The man's horse rested near the open doorway and Fargo moved closer and heard the sounds coming from inside the house. He had moved into the clearing and was approaching the house when the figure came through the doorway, a saddlebag slung over one shoulder. The man halted, surprise in his narrow face as he saw the big man with the Colt aimed at him.

"Drop the saddlebag," Fargo said, and the man obeyed. "Now the gunbelt," Fargo said. The man took another glance at the Colt and unbuckled his gunbelt. "Now move back, into the shack," Fargo ordered as the gunbelt dropped to the ground. The man stepped backward through the doorway and Fargo followed him into the shack. His quick glance took in four mattresses along with piles of clothes and leather sacks. This was where they had holed up while they waited and watched the town. He was certain of the answer to the question, but he still had to ask it. "Who sent you?" he thrust at the man.

"Kale," the man said, his narrow face twitching.

"How long have you been here?"

"About a month," the man said, and Fargo nodded with grim satisfaction. Kale had begun making moves the moment he learned Joanna had sent for Fargo.

"Let's go," Fargo said. "Some other folks will have questions for you." He stepped aside and the man walked past him through the doorway. Fargo followed him outside as the man walked toward his horse. "Take the reins and walk him," Fargo said, and keeping the Colt in hand, began to move from the clearing to where he had left the Ovaro. The man had reached his horse and started to take hold of the reins when suddenly he whirled and Fargo saw the gun come out from inside his shirt. Fargo dived to his left as the man fired, the bullet hurtling behind his back. He hit the ground, rolled, heard another shot slam into the dirt, and brought the Colt up as he rolled to a stop. He fired from an almost supine position and saw the man's body double forward as the heavy slug ripped through his midsection.

Fargo fired again as the man started to go down, saw his body quiver as it hit the ground and then lay still, curled in almost a fetal position. Fargo stood up and walked to where the man lay, the gun still clutched in his hand, a Colt House pistol, a four-shot, single-action gun only a little larger than a derringer. The man wouldn't be answering any more questions. Fargo turned and walked back into the shack. Maybe he could find a few answers in there.

He began to look through the scattered clothes and canvas sacks and one caught his eye, longer and larger than the others. He pulled the top open to stare down at the contents and frowned. He opened another sack nearby and spilled its contents on the floor. A wry sound escaped his lips. Answers came in all sorts of packages. Tying the two sacks together, he lifted them over one shoulder and strode from the cabin. When he reached the Ovaro he slung the sacks from the saddlehorn and rode back to Snow Bow, where he found Nugget watching two men load the three slain ambushers onto a flat-bed wagon while a handful of onlookers stood by.

"The town burying folks," Nugget said. "Gave them a five-dollar gold piece."

"What about the sheriff?" Fargo asked.

"They don't have one," Nugget said. "What about your man? He get away?"

"He got dead," Fargo said, pausing as the two men

clambered onto the wagon and drove away. "Let's get back," he said, and Nugget went to the rear of the building and returned on the gray mare.

"You did well," Fargo said as Nugget rode beside him, and the old miner nodded in quiet satisfaction. He rode in silence and Fargo smiled. The years teach a man patience.

There were but a few hours left to the night when they reached the campsite, but Fargo saw Glory sit up at once and, a moment later, Joanna push up onto her elbows. Both watched as he put the sacks on the ground and unsaddled the pinto, and they lay back only when he went into the trees with his bedroll.

He slept soundly till he woke with the morning birdsongs, used his canteen to wash, and went back to where the others were camped. Both Joanna and Glory were up and dressed. Joanna came to him. "I didn't sleep much last night, thanks to you," she said. "What happened?" He told her everything as it had unfolded and saw Glory come up to listen, Nugget behind her.

"I followed one to where they'd been living while they took turns watching the town," he said. "They were Kale's men. He told me that before he got cute."

"He tell you anything else?" Joanna questioned.

"He didn't but some of their things did," Fargo said, and stepped toward the two sacks he had brought back. He turned both over and emptied their contents on the ground, reached down and picked up two objects. One was a tin can whose top portion had been fashioned into a long, thin spout, the other a bottle fitted with a leather jacket from which a long-curved hook protruded. A cork was in the top of the bottle. "You know what these are?" Fargo asked.

"No," Joanna said.

"These are lubricant holders. Every logger carries one. They hold the lubricant, usually kerosene, that thins the sticky pitch that builds up on saw blades. The hook holds the can onto the tree and the lubricant is poured through the thin spout or a notched cork. No logger can saw for long without his lubricant can," Fargo said. He set down the two containers and picked up the next object.

"That's a saw. Anybody can see that," Joanna said.

"But not an ordinary saw," Fargo told her, and ran his fingers casually over the unevenly spaced teeth of the blade. "This is a bucking saw. It has a cross-cut blade and it's used to cut up the big trees that have been downed. It's made so it can be used by two men at once." Fargo picked up a tangle of heavy rope, pulleys, and blocks. "Equipment used by the high climbers and spar men. Loggers' equipment, all of it. That say anything to you?" Joanna frowned, uncertainty clouding her face.

"Duncan Kale didn't go gold mining," Fargo said. "He bought himself a logging operation. These were men *he* sent. Their tools were those of loggers, not gold miners."

Joanna's eyes held Fargo's for a long moment as his words sank in, and then she looked down at the objects on the ground. "That bastard," she breathed. "That no good, rotten bastard."

"Maybe there's a good side," Fargo said.

Joanna's eyes flashed fury. "I'd like to hear that," she bit out.

"I don't have to wonder about a passel of gold-mine areas. The way he headed he had to be going only one place, north into the high logging country in Idaho and Washington," Fargo said.

Joanna's lips pursed and her eyes narrowed as she

looked at him. "Then let's go, damn it. I want Duncan Kale, wherever he is."

"Get saddled," Fargo said, and his eyes found Glory. "Kale sent them to kill me. I guess that takes care of your thinking that they were after Evie that night," he said.

"Hell it does," Glory snapped. "Because he sent these men to kill you doesn't prove he sent the ones that killed Evie."

Fargo saw Joanna pause to cast a disdainful glance at Glory. "You still going to cling to that ridiculous idea? After this?" She frowned. "Can't you say you were wrong?"

"I'll say it when I'm sure of it. This didn't make me sure," Glory said tersely, and walked away. Joanna looked after her for a moment, disdain still in her eyes, then walked to her horse. Fargo met Nugget's eyes and the older miner shrugged.

"You siding with her?" Fargo growled.

"No, but I can't positively say she's wrong, not yet," Nugget said.

"She's like a damn dog with a bone. She won't let go if it."

"Maybe in time," Nugget said.

"She'll have time. It'll be slow riding from here, right through the Bitteroot Range north," Fargo said. "I want you to leave all that gold-mining equipment you brought. Take these loggers' tools instead. We want to look the part when we get there."

"Yes, that's for sure," Nugget said as he hurried off.

They were all ready to go within a half hour and Fargo's prediction quickly came true as he led the way through winding passages that rose up sharply to fall away with equal sharpness. By afternoon he found a few moose and deer trails that were worn enough to make riding easier. Joanna dropped back to ride with Gus Harby for a while, and when Fargo halted to rest the horses she came up to him.

"The men would like some fresh meat. They'd like to shoot some of the rabbits that are all over the place," she said.

"White-tailed jacks," Fargo grunted. "Tell them to shoot enough for everybody. I'll find a spot to bed down within the hour to allow time for skinning."

"Great," she said, and returned to where Harby and the others rested. For the next hour, the way northward was punctuated by rifle shots and the sound of riders pushing through the brush to retrieve their prizes. Fargo found a small arbor set in a high hollow while the sun was just starting to dip behind the taller peaks, and called a halt. Four small cooking fires were started. Two of the men were good skinners and the rabbits were roasting on makeshift spits before the dark came. The hot fires did their job quickly and Fargo sat back as the others ate. There was plenty of rabbit left when he rose and started for the fire. Nugget appeared at the roast just as he did.

"Where's Glory?" Fargo asked.

"Being a damn female, stubborn and ornery."

"What's that mean?"

"She won't come eat, that's what," Nugget said. "She's over there against the balsam."

Fargo strode in the direction Nugget indicated and was quickly enveloped in darkness, but the fire cast enough glow for him to discern the slender figure sitting against the tree. She looked up at him as he stopped.

"How old did you say you were?" he asked.

"Shove it, Fargo!"

"Then why are you acting like a six-year-old?"

"Her men shot it. Her food. Her show. I've my own things," Glory said.

"She asked me if they could go shooting. I said yes. That makes it my decision. Now get something to eat. Some hot, fresh meat will be good for you. That's an order," he said.

She waited a minute before standing up. "If it's an order," she said finally, and walked to the fire. He followed, cut a thick slice of rabbit for her and one for himself and walked back to the balsam with her.

"Doesn't take much for you to get your nose out of joint, does it?" he remarked. "She's got a right to disagree with you, same as I have."

"It's not being disagreed with, it's being looked down on. It's her way. She doesn't care about anybody," Glory said.

"Ever think you're a mite thin-skinned?" Fargo said, his tone gentle.

"Ever think you're a mite blind?" Glory said not at all gently.

"Can't say that I have." Fargo laughed. "Get some sleep. Riding won't get any easier tomorrow."

The fires were put out, the rabbit bones buried, and the camp settled down. Fargo had just taken up his bedroll when Joanna appeared, circling the edge of the site. She came up to stand close in front of him, her voice a whisper.

"I'm exhausted. I meant it about not sleeping last night. It was from worrying about you," she said. "I still think it was a damn-fool thing to do."

"That's your right," Fargo said blandly.

"But you turned what could've been disaster into something great. You stopped us from going on a wild goose chase after gold-mining operations. You are something special," she said.

"Flattery will get you anywhere." He grinned.

"Not flattery, just truth," she said. She reached up and pressed her lips to his, a quick, soft kiss. "Thank you," she said, pulled away, and quickly hurried into the darkness. Fargo took his bedroll into the woods and found a spot beside a red fir. He felt his own tiredness pull at him. He slept in minutes after undressing and woke only when the new day filtered through the trees.

The day's ride proved just as slow and difficult as the day before, and the high mountains of the Bitterroot Range rose up on all sides of them as they plunged into the heart of the rugged terrain. A swift-running mountain stream offered a spot to rest and refresh the horses a little past midday. He found himself beside Glory as she plunged her face into the cooling water. Her slim body dipped and bent and then straightened, all with supple grace, her little breasts moving in unison under the blue shirt she wore. She patted her face dry and met his appreciative gaze, her face relaxed, a soft prettiness in it.

"Glad you've got your nose back in joint," he remarked.

"Haven't changed my mind about anything I said," she returned.

"Didn't expect that." Fargo laughed.

"I know she's been telling you how concerned she was for you the other night," Glory said as she got to her feet.

"Nothing wrong with that, is there?"

"No. But some people worry without thinking so much about it," she said, and hurried away.

"Thanks," he called after her, but she didn't glance back. He smiled as he rose and climbed onto the pinto. Her words had held layered meanings, the implication that silence showed greater sincerity than speech. Maybe sometimes, he conceded, but often it only indicated different personalities with different ways. Glory had too much resentment in her to see that. He waved an arm at the others and led the way down a steep pass between two high, spruce-covered crags.

They were deeper and higher into the mountain fastness when the day began to draw to an end. A few dozen yards ahead of the others, Fargo reined to a halt to peer at the terrain in front of him. A towering mountain rose, forbidding in its very size. Alone one side a path circled its rock-bound denseness, a path only wide enough for a single horse and rider. On one side the path clung to the mountain, which rose up straight with rock and brush. On the other side a sheer cliff dropped away to end a thousand feet below in a bed of jagged rocks. He was still peering at the narrow path as the others came up and Joanna drew alongside him. "Oh, God," she murmured in dismay.

"It's the only way unless we drop back and try to circle the mountain. That could take us a week or more," he said.

Joanna frowned. "I don't want that."

"We can make it if we go single file and real slow," Fargo said as his glance moved up the curving, narrow path. "But it's too late to even think of starting now. I wouldn't want to be caught there when night falls."

"Good God no," Joanna murmured.

Fargo turned his eyes to the right and spotted a hollow surrounded by juniper-covered rises. "We'll bed down there for the night and tackle that mountain come morning," he said, and led the way downward to the sweet-smelling hollow that proved larger than it had seemed from a distance. They reached it just before night began to drop over the high peaks. The ground had only barren grass cover; plenty of deer tracks told him why.

Tiredness made everyone eat quickly and silently, and a full moon rose to bathe the mountains in a pale light. Fargo let everyone settle down before he rose with his bedroll, pausing to glance across the hollow again. Joanna lay alone beside a big red fir, Nugget curled up a few yards away, and he found Glory near the old miner, her saddle alongside her. Fargo started into the trees and climbed a low slope. He'd gone only a few dozen steps when he heard the sound of someone following. He turned to see Joanna, her blue robe wrapped around her, and waited as she came up to him. "Go on, find a spot," she murmured, and walked beside him as he went on, halting beside a blue spruce where the ground lay covered with a bed of soft broom moss.

He dropped the bedroll on the ground, spread it out as Joanna watched. "Something more you want to tell me?" he asked as he took off his gunbelt.

"No, I did all my talking last night," she said as her hand came up and pulled her robe open. She wore a nightgown under it, loose at the top, and she shook her shoulders and the gown fell to her waist. Fargo's gaze held on her full-fleshed torso, creamy breasts deep and full and very round, each topped with a dark pink nipple centered on a large pink areola. A few extra pounds gave her less than a narrow waistline but added to her air of mature pliancy. Her hands pushed on the nightgown and it slid over ample hips to fall to the ground. Joanna stepped forward. Fargo took in rounded hips and thighs that just avoided being heavy, a convex little belly, and under it a very dense, very black triangle.

Her hands came up and began to unbutton his shirt, and he smelled the faintly musky odor of her, a mingling of powder and body scent, instantly exciting. He felt himself responding at once. She pushed his shirt from him as he undid trousers and kicked off boots. Her breasts came to press into his chest with wonderful softness. He sank onto the bedroll and pulled her with him and she came down over him, pressing her breasts into his face with sweet smothering. Joanna lay tight against him as he found one deep breast with his lips, caressed the firm pink tip, drew it into his mouth and pulled on it. "Ah, aaaah," she murmured, and turned with him as he rolled her onto her back. His mouth pulled from her breast and found her lips— soft, enveloping lips made for sensual pleasures.

Joanna's moan came from deep inside her as his hands caressed her breasts, circled each nipple, gently touched the tips that now had grown into soft firmness. He ran both hands down across her waist, slow tracings against the hotness of her skin, pressed them to her hips, and moved inward to knead the convexity of her belly. His hands slid downward, fingers pushing through the very dense, very black triangle, the wiry touch of it exciting. He pressed against the soft rise of her pubic mound and Joanna's moan deepened. Her full-fleshed thighs opened and her dense triangle and her moan became a gasped cry. She opened her thighs further, moved her hips from side to side.

"Come to me, Jesus, come to me, Fargo . . ." she whispered, and her hands were pressing into his buttocks, pulling him to her. He half-rose, let himself come forward, and her thighs clamped around him, a vise of hotness, the eternal invitation of the flesh. "Oh, oooooaaaah," Joanna groaned as he touched the wet, warm pathway. Her groan rose, became a half-scream of delight as he slid forward. Her legs clasped together around his thighs, pushing him deeper, and her arms encircled his neck to pull his face down to the deep, enveloping breasts. Joanna drew her body in, pulled it back, and slid forward with a great, gasping groan, moving in slow rhythm to his sliding thrusts.

No quivering, intense pleasure for her but a consuming, deep fire, an enveloping intensity, an inner echo of the enveloping softness of her breasts. She groaned words, stretching each one out in a deep gasp that matched her slow, sliding motions. "Yes, ye-e-e-s-s-s . . . aaaaah . . . more . . . mo-o-ore," she breathed, and he moved more quickly inside her. She lifted her hips, surged upward to match his rhythm, her movements not unlike the rolling of a slow wave onto the beach, fluid movement cresting to a moaning break and then receding only to surge forward again. He caught the change in the low moaning sounds first, then felt the quickening of her surges, her soft thighs pressing tighter. Then he was being carried along on a deep turbulence, her large breasts jiggling, her low sounds now almost angry groans. "Oh, damn, oh, damn . . . ah, ah, aaaaaaaah, yes, Jesus yes," Joanna gasped. He felt himself carried over the sweet edge with her, plunging into her moaning ecstasy, feeling throbbing explosions of his own, whirlwinds of the flesh commingling until, with a groaning shudder, she fell back, suddenly limp.

He stayed with her, rested atop her, still enveloped by her soft warmth, until finally he drew back and lay beside her. She turned on her side, one arm around his waist, the deep breasts warm and pillowy against him. "You'll remember this the next time I don't want you to do something. You'll remember that I want you, that I care. Words don't last. Actions last."

"I'll remember," Fargo said. "But I won't promise."

Her smile was smug. "I'll settle for remembering . . . for now," she said. She put her head against his shoulder, the warm, soft breasts half over his chest, and closed her eyes, enveloping him even as she slept. He pulled the bedroll over her, settled himself down, and let the warm night bring sleep.

5

He was sitting atop the Ovaro, staring at the mountain and the narrow path that curved around it, when the others arrived. Joanna had left his bedroll but a few minutes before dawn crept over the high peaks and he had come down to the camp while the others still slept. It was Glory who rode up a few moments before anyone else, her voice cutting into his thoughts. "I told them you'd be here," she said, faint disapproval in her voice. "They were all wondering where you were."

"How'd you know?" he asked, his eyes still on the mountain path.

"You're the trailsman. You'd be here sure as a fox would be at a chicken coop," she said, and his wry smile held concession. She was right. The others came up and Joanna halted beside him, her glance quick but with a private smile in her eyes.

"Give me a few minutes to take a closer look, then come on," he told her, and set off in a canter across the few hundred yards to the mountain. He reached the bottom of the narrow path and peered upward, dismounted, and began to walk its precarious roadway. His eyes measured curvature, steepness, and width, and he finally halted and knelt. Pressing his hands to the edge of the path, he peered down at the jagged rocks below the almost sheer drop, repeated the test at half a dozen other places and finally walked back down to the base of the mountain and rode to where the others waited. "It seems to stay the same width as far as I can see," he told them. "The cliff edge is firm enough."

"Single file, of course," Joanna said.

"That's right. It's wide enough for you to dismount if you want to lead your horse for a spell but that's all. There's not enough room to turn around, and backing up is out. Once we're on it we have to keep going till we reach the top," Fargo said. "You all be slow and careful and we can do it." His glance moved across the others and he saw some of the men peer uneasily at the dangerous pathway. "Anyone want to back out this is the time to do it," he said.

"Anyone who backs out doesn't get paid," Joanna's voice cut in sharply. No one answered and Fargo turned the Ovaro toward the narrow path. He led the way upward and glanced back to see that Joanna had swung in behind him. Glory followed, Nugget behind her, and Gus Harby and his men made up the rest of the procession. Fargo walked the Ovaro, glancing down at the cliff from time to time as he kept the horse hugging the mountainside. The cliff grew deeper as they climbed, the pathway growing steep in places. It was a trail for mountain goats, Fargo grumbled silently, and cast another glance behind. Joanna had fallen back a few paces as she moved the roan with careful slowness.

It was midday, the sun burning, when they reached halfway up the path, and Fargo raised a hand as he reined to a halt. The path ahead grew sharply steeper. "Rest your horses," he called back, and very carefully swung from the saddle to stand in the narrow space between the horse and the cliff edge of the path. He had not much more than a foot of space, he saw, and moved to stand in front of the pinto. Some of the others were dismounting, Joanna among them. "Stand in front of your horses," he called quickly. "They take a half-step sideways and they'll knock you off." He saw the others hasten to obey. He sank down to rest on one knee as Joanna precariously edged her way to him. She peered up at the steepness of the path, her eyes narrowed.

"Good idea, resting the horses," she said. "We can make it."

"We've no choice now," Fargo muttered grimly. He let another fifteen minutes go by and rose to his feet. Joanna blew him a surreptitious kiss as she carefully siddled her way back to the roan. Fargo took equally careful steps as he trod the edge of the path before swinging back onto the Ovaro. He moved forward and felt the horse's powerful hindquarter muscles grow tight as the climb grew suddenly steeper. He leaned forward in the saddle to balance his weight, letting the horse set its own pace. The path continued upwards steeply and he concentrated on keeping the horse away from the edge, using only the lightest touch of the reins.

They had climbed some ten minutes, a heavy line of perspiration forming on his brow, when the tense silence suddenly shattered, Glory's voice spiraling skyward in terror. His head swiveled just in time to see her disappear over the cliff edge, her saddle tumbling after her.

"Damn!" Fargo swore as he halted and slid from the saddle, forcing himself to move carefully. Glory's scream had ended abruptly, too abruptly, and he felt hope leap inside him as he reached the cliffside. He saw her, some twenty feet below, lodged on a protuberance of rock that jutted from the otherwise sheer cliff. A gnarled and twisted limb, a stunted piece of hackberry, grew almost horizontally from a crevice in the cliffside, and part of Glory's body was wedged against it. The saddle had caught at the edge of the gnarled limb to hang there looking obscenely inappropriate.

Fargo moved back to the Ovaro and got his lariat, edged his way past Joanna, who swung from the roan as soon as he went by. "What are you going to do?"

"See if I can reach her," Fargo said.

Joanna peered over the edge of the cliff. "You can't do it. There's not more than two feet of space," she said.

"I've got to try," Fargo said, looking up at Nugget, who still sat the gray mare. "What happened?" he asked.

"She suddenly fell. The saddle gave way," Nugget said. "I was watching my mare's steps when suddenly Glory screamed. I looked up and she and the saddle were going over the side. I couldn't even get a hand on her."

Some of the men had dismounted to stand with their horses and Fargo saw Joanna looking over the cliff edge again. "She hasn't moved," Joanna said.

"Thank God for that," Fargo said. "She wakes up groggy and she'll sure as hell go over the rest of the way." His gaze swept the rocks that formed the mountainside next to the narrow path, then halted at a jagged spur of granite that jutted out and upward. He took two steps and wrapped one end of the lariat around the spur, jammed it down into the crevice, took two more turns around the rock and then stepped back to the edge.

He felt Joanna's hand on his arm. "She may be dead, Fargo. She could have broken her neck. You're risking your life, maybe for nothing," she said.

"Not for nothing. For that word 'maybe,' " Fargo said. He clasped both hands around the lariat and swung over the side. The line of heads peered down at him from the path as he began to lower himself, quickly at first, then slowing. The protuberance of rock appeared just below him, the space in it even smaller than it had seemed from above. He touched down on the balls of his feet, coiled the lariat around himself twice. There was just enough room for him to get down to one knee beside her. She was unconscious but she was breathing, he saw, a bruise on her temple. He risked reaching out with one hand, moved her head from side to side. It moved freely, nothing broken, and he allowed himself a surge of hope.

He raised his head and looked upward toward the path above and saw that the cliff veered outward before it dropped off again. She had hit against the cliff where it veered out, a glancing blow but enough to break her fall before she landed on the protuberance of rock. Fargo's eyes went to the saddle where it continued to hang, swaying slightly from the end of the gnarled growth of hackberry. Moving slowly, he reached out again and managed to pull Glory up almost to a sitting position. He grimaced as he saw his right foot half over the edge of the tiny rock shelf. There was no room for mistakes. One misstep could send Glory plunging down, this time with nothing to stop her fall.

His lips tight, he slowly began to pull her limp figure

toward him with one hand as, with the other, he uncoiled the lariat from around himself and lifted it over her head. He let it fall to her waist and then pulled it tight. Working with his heart in his mouth, he wrapped the rest of the rope around himself and Glory until he had her bound hard against him. He rose, cursing as he felt his foot slip off the tiny shelf, but managed to keep his balance. He began to pull himself upward along the lariat, Glory's limp form bound to him. He had climbed only a few feet when he felt the pain in his arms, starting in his forearms, sliding up into his upper arms and then into the knotted muscles of his shoulders.

He paused, managed to extend his legs enough to press his feet against the rock wall and rest for a moment. Gathering new breath and the determination to ignore muscles that had begun to burn with pain, he pulled upward again and heard his whispered curses. Glory's limp form was slipping down from the coiled rope that bound them together. He renewed his efforts and now his curses were no longer whispered but savage gasps he flung into the air.

Pausing again, he craned his stiffened neck upward and saw he was but a few feet from the top. Nugget's face peered down at him, Joanna's beside him, some of the others crowded nearby. "Get back. Move the horses. We can't spook the horses," he called out, surprised at the strength left in his voice. The faces disappeared from view and he heard the sounds of the horses being led up the path. He began to pull again, cursing the pain of it, but suddenly he felt the edge of the cliff. He kept pulling, moved his body and Glory past the edge before he swung in and lay gasping on the path, gulping in deep drafts of air. He could see that Nugget and Joanna had moved their horses up the path while Gus Harby and the others stayed where they were, and he felt hands loosening the lariat, lifting the loops over his head.

Nugget was on one knee beside him pulling Glory further up on the path as Fargo shook his head and pushed to his knees. Glory lay on her back and Fargo carefully moved her limbs, legs first, then her arms. "Nothing's broken," he muttered as he felt the terrible burning in his own muscles begin to lessen. He sat beside Glory as she lay stretched out on the narrow path. He was the first to see her eyelids flutter. A soft moan followed and her eyelids fluttered again, slowly came open. She started to roll over and he pressed her back with one hand. "Easy," he said, and met her eyes as they stared at him, awakening slowly coming into their dark blue depths.

"Oh, God," she breathed. "Oh, my God," and her arms were around his neck, her body quivering as she clung to him. Finally she pulled away, her small breasts pushing hard against her shirt as she drew in a deep, long breath.

"You were damn lucky," he said.

"Lucky that you were here."

"Lucky the ledge was there."

"Both," she murmured.

"Can you stand?" he asked, and she nodded. He rose and pulled her to her feet; she swayed for a moment and then straightened. "What happened?" he asked.

"I don't know. The saddle fell from the bay and took me with it," she said. "The cinch must've snapped."

"More likely you didn't tie it right," Fargo said. "It worked itself loose with the pressure of mountain riding."

"I tied it right. I always tie it the same way," she said.

"Not this time. You probably didn't get the latigo pulled

97

tight enough through the cinch ring. I've seen them come loose before," he said.

"It broke. The damn strap broke," Glory said, and he shrugged. The answer was a possibility. He stepped to the cliff edge and peered down at the saddle, still hanging on the gnarled trunk.

"I'll go back down and get the saddle if I can," he said.

"No!" Joanna's voice cut in. "You risked getting killed once. You're not doing it again for a damn saddle."

"She can't ride bareback through these mountains," Fargo said. "She's going to need a saddle."

Joanna moved away as she beckoned to him, stepping carefully along the edge of the narrow pathway. He followed to where she halted, out of earshot of the others. Her voice was a whisper. "I thought last night meant something. I thought you understood."

"I do, but I told you there'd be no promises," he said.

"Damn it, Fargo, we'll rig up some kind of saddle for her," Joanna hissed.

"That's impossible. I don't think the latigo strap broke. I think she didn't tie it right. But if it did, I can rig up another strap. I can't rig up a saddle," he said.

Joanna gazed down over the edge. "Maybe you could get a lasso around it from up here," she said.

"Never. I'd just jar it loose and it'd go down," Fargo said. "I've got to get closer. I can do it." He turned from her and stepped back to where Glory waited, her back against the wall edge of the path. She came forward at once to throw her arms around him.

"Thank you. God, thank you," she murmured. "I don't think I said it before."

"Some things don't need saying," he told her as Joanna's voice cut in.

"Save the gratitude for your own time," she snapped. "This is a dangerous place. I want to get off it before we have another accident."

Fargo shrugged. "You're right," he said. Once again he wrapped the lariat around his waist and started to lower himself over the edge. His muscles protested immediately, but less severely than before, and he reached the little rock protuberance. His eyes narrowed as he surveyed the saddle where it hung precariously at the end of the twisted limb. The rock ledge hadn't room enough for him to get the right angle to toss the lariat over the center of the saddle. His only chance was to get closer to it from behind, and that meant along the almost horizontal tree limb.

His lips pulled back in a grimace, he pressed both hands against the base of the limb where it grew out of the rock crevice. He pushed carefully, cursed as he saw the saddle sway at once. But the limb seemed sturdy enough and he unwrapped the lariat from around his waist and stretched out prone across the base of the limb. He began to crawl, six inches at a time, and felt the limb dip as more of his weight came onto it. But it only dipped an inch or so, and he was more concerned with the sway of the saddle. Holding the end of the lariat in his right hand, the loop extended downward, he moved forward again, and cursed as he saw the saddle begin to dip. It could tear loose at any moment, he knew, and he halted. He was halfway out along the tree and he wrapped both legs around the limb, tightening his thigh muscles to keep a firm grip on the precarious perch. He let his right arm swing loosely, back and forth, letting the rope take on momentum, the loop of the lariat still held downward. And then, with a quick but smooth motion, he lifted the loop and sent it flying forward.

Holding his breath, he saw it close over the front of the saddle, drop down below the horn and over the seat. The saddle tore loose but the lasso was around it as it fell. He felt the weight of it almost pull him from the limb as his body flipped over, and now he was hanging by his legs from the bottom of the limb. But he had hold of the saddle, which felt as though it were going to pull his arm from his shoulder socket. He reached his other arm up, got a grip around the tree limb and, using his one arm and his legs tightly wrapped around the limb, began to inch his way backward to the rock shelf.

He finally reached it, only a few feet that had seemed more like a thousand yards, let his upper body fall onto the rock and then disengaged his legs and drew them up. He rested a minute before he turned onto his stomach and began to pull the saddle up. He drew it onto the rock ledge and lay back again until his breath returned to something near normal. He had always wished a saddle could be lighter and now he swore it was time for someone to invent one. He pushed to his feet, wrapped the saddle against himself with coils of the lariat, much as he had with Glory, and once again began the pull up the side of the cliff. His muscles were burning again when he reached the top and Nugget's hands helped pull him and the cumbersome saddle over the edge.

He rested a moment and finally rose. He saw Gus Harby watching with admiration. "You're something special, mister," the man said. Fargo's eyes found Joanna, up a dozen feet along the path beside her horse.

She refused to concede anything, her face tight as she turned away. He shrugged inwardly. She'd come around, he was certain. The rear jockey and skirt had remained on Glory's horse when the saddle gave way, and Fargo rose, lifted the saddle, and flung it onto the horse. "I'll look at it later," he muttered. "Let's get the hell off this mountain." He shot a glance at Glory where she waited at the head of her roan. "Lead him," he said, and tossed a glance at the others. "Nothing's changed. Slow and easy."

He edged past Glory and found himself alongside Joanna, who shot him a hurt glance. "I feel as if last night was a waste," she said.

"Nothing that much fun is ever a waste, honey," he said cheerfully, and edged on to the Ovaro. He let a weary sigh escape him and climbed onto the horse. He peered up the slow curve of the path. It seemed endless; he only hoped that they'd reach the top without another accident. He set a slow and careful pace, glanced back often to see Joanna behind him, her face still set. Glory walked close after her, pulling the roan along by the reins, and he saw Nugget mopping his face often as he showed the effect of the searing sun. But the others behind him, forty years younger, were showing the same effect. Fargo concentrated on the climb and swore softly as the path grew even narrower as they rode higher. He swore harder as he saw the sun beginning to edge behind the peaks. They had another hour before the day ended, he estimated, but he didn't dare quicken the pace. Tired riders and tired horses were a combination made for missteps.

But the day drew inexorably toward an end. They had not more than another ten minutes of light left and the path curved sharply. It was impossible to see how much of it still rose ahead. He had already decided that when the blackness of night descended they would halt, everyone would dismount and stay in place, and they'd wait till the moon rose high enough to send down some light they could use. It posed a real risk, he realized. It'd take at least an hour, maybe two, for the moon to rise high enough. The horses were the danger. They were tired, and tired horses were easily spooked—a wolf's howl, a sudden flurry of night-bird wings, anything could set them off. If one spooked it would set off a chain reaction. If one fell, others would rear up and surely go over the edge.

He grew sick at the very real danger of it happening even as he knew it would be equally suicidal to go on in the blackness. He rode upward with his mouth a grim line across his face, one eye on the last of the sun edging behind a peak. He had just rounded the last of a sharp curve when he felt the shout rise up in his throat. The path ended with breathtaking abruptness, flattening out onto a high mountain plateau. "Hallelujah," Fargo called back as he sent the pinto into a canter for the last hundred yards. The plateau was a terrain of open space and quaking aspen along with a sprinkling of red fir, and he glanced back to see the others hurrying onto the flat land, Joanna leading the bay to one side. Night was desending and Fargo gestured to ana open space against a line of aspen. "We'll bed down right here," he said, and the others were quick to find a spot and unsaddle their horses.

It was almost dark when he stepped to where Glory had halted, and he swung the saddle to the ground. "We'll have a look at it come morning," he said, and she nodded as she sank to the ground.

"I'm too exhausted to do anything but sleep," she said, words echoed by everyone else as they fell in silent weariness to the grass. Fargo took his bedroll off to the far end of the trees, paused where Joanna had settled down.

"You going to keep on pouting?" he asked.

"There's a difference between pouting and hurting," she said.

"There's a difference in doing something because you want to and putting strings on it," he said evenly. She didn't answer and he moved on, found a spot at the far end of the area, undressed and sank down on his bedroll. He felt the ache of every muscle in his body and he was asleep in minutes, too exhausted to hear the sound of a pair of noisy raccoons only a few feet away.

6

His body held him a prisoner past sunrise, but the others were still asleep when he rose. After he washed and dressed he walked to where he had put Glory's saddle, and felt a moment of surprise when he saw her coming out of the trees toward him. She was fully dressed and looking crisply slender in a tan shirt and Levi's. "You look at it yet?" she asked.

"No," he said. "You?"

"No," she said, dropping to her knees beside him as he began to examine the saddle. He turned it half over and ran his hand along the latigo strap. "It's all in one piece," he said, and did the same with the rigging straps. "Nothing broken there, either," he said, more smugly than he'd intended, and saw Glory's eyes flash at once.

"I didn't tie it too loose. Something broke," she insisted.

Fargo shrugged, pulled the saddle closer, and examined the cinch. He frowned as he ran his hand along the band leading to the cinch ring. The cinch ring wasn't there.

He reached down and pulled the latigo strap to him again and found the cinch ring hanging from the end of it.

"What is it?" Glory asked, reading his face.

"The cinch tore loose," he said.

"Impossible!" Glory snapped.

"No, I've seen them do that when they're frayed," Fargo told her.

"It wasn't frayed. I looked it over before we started this trip."

Fargo held the end of the cinch up to the cinch ring. "It's frayed right here," he said and then the words froze in his mouth. He stared at the wide band where it normally held the cinch ring. Only the last half-inch was pulled loose and frayed, the ends hanging raggedly. The rest of the cinch was a sharp, clean line. "It was cut," Fargo breathed. "Goddamn, it was cut. Just enough was left for it to tear loose by itself with the pressure of climbing."

"My God," Glory said, her voice a whisper. "No accident. Someone wanted me killed."

Fargo's lips tightened. "It sure seems that way."

"This proves it, don't you see?" Glory said.

"Proves what?"

"That they were out to kill Evie that night, not you. They were afraid of what she might tell you, and now they're trying for me."

"But you said Evie hadn't told you anything," Fargo said.

"They don't know that. They're taking no chances," Glory answered.

Fargo's lips tightened again. Evie had been the target that night. It pulled together now, at least that much of it. "Who, damn it?" he asked Glory. "Think back. Think about some little thing Evie might've said. Who doesn't care if I go after Kale but is so afraid of something Evie might have known?''

"I've thought plenty about that. I don't know. I can't come up with anyone or anything," Glory said.

Fargo grimaced at the thought that flared inside him. "They slipped someone in with the men Joanna hired," he murmured. Glory's face was grave as she nodded. The others were beginning to wake, Fargo saw, and glimpsed Joanna's blue robe as she went into the trees. "You keep quiet about this," he told Glory. "I'll talk to Joanna." Glory nodded again and he left her. He began to saddle the Ovaro as the others slowly rose. Finally Joanna returned, her full breasts pressing hard against a white blouse. He beckoned to her and drew her aside. "The accident was no accident," he said.

Joanna stared at him. "What are you talking about?" she asked. He began to tell her what he had discovered and her stare became one of utter disbelief. When he finished, she continued to stare at him in silence. "Are you sure?" she finally asked.

"Too damn sure," Fargo muttered savagely. "How'd you hire your men?" he asked.

"I put signs up in the general store and the saloon. They said I was looking for help," Joanna told him. "I picked the men I wanted from those who showed up."

"Signs," Fargo murmured. "Probably everybody in town saw them."

"Probably," Joanna agreed.

"It would've been easy to plant somebody, easy as eating apple pie," Fargo thought aloud.

"Yes, I suppose so," Joanna said regretfully.

"I've got to find out who it is."

"That's impossible," she said. "Unless he tries something again."

"It might be too late then. We can't go on knowing he could strike again. Maybe I can't find him, but I've got to try," Fargo said.

"How?"

"That cinch was cut through very carefully. It took time. He wouldn't have dared do it with the saddle lying alongside Glory. That means he had to carry it away, do it, and then bring it back. Maybe he left something I can use—a button, a piece of torn shirt, a footprint," Fargo said.

"Go all the way down and come back again? That'll take you all day," Joanna said, and he nodded. "For nothing, most likely. I say we go on and just keep alert. Time is important, Fargo."

"So's life," he said. "I won't give him another chance unless I can't help it. Everybody can stand a day's rest after that climb yesterday. That's all I'll need, one day. If I can find something, I'll know who it is. If not, we go on."

"I'm not happy," Joanna said. "You're going on a wild goose chase."

"Sorry you're not happy. Meanwhile, go tell the others you've decided to rest a day. I'll just disappear," he said.

Joanna's face reflected her displeasure as she turned away and started to walk toward the others. Fargo took the Ovaro, drew into the trees, and moved quickly along the edge of the plateau. He reached the mountain path and decided he'd make better time walking down and riding back. He set off down the path and the Ovaro followed with ease without the weight of a rider. Fargo walked fast, made good time, and reached the bottom of the path soon after the sun had swung into the early afternoon. He made his way to where they had camped within sight of the mountain path and grunted in satisfaction. The ground, he'd remembered rightly, was only barren grass cover, with more than ample soil for footprints.

He walked carefully around the perimeter of the area and found the red fir where Joanna had bedded down. Nugget had been only a half-dozen yards to her left. Fargo moved sideways and then on to where Glory had slept. He halted, the marks faint but still there in the soil. He knelt and found the slight indentations in the soil where the saddle had rested, the imprint of the stirrups still clear. His gaze moved slowly as it separated the slurred footprints that were all over the ground. Finally he found the ones he sought, a pair of footprints that moved in a straight line from where the saddle had rested.

He rose, followed to where the prints halted against the trees. The man had carried the saddle there, put it down on the ground again while he worked on the cinch. Fargo's eyes were hard as blue agate as he scanned each footprint, and his jaw throbbed as he found something he could use. The heel of the man's right boot had a chip out of it. He grunted. Not a lot but enough. The footprint it left carried the mark, clear enough to spot. But he'd have to be careful, he knew. He couldn't be obvious. He'd lie back, watch and wait. Patience. The footprint would turn up and he'd have his attempted killer.

He straightened up, walked back to the pinto, and swung onto the saddle. He let the horse set its own pace as he started back up the narrow mountain path, but the climb back took considerably longer than it had on the way down. It took even longer as the darkness fell and he rode hugging the right side of the path. When he finally reached the top where it became the narrow high plateau the night had grown still. As he drew near the campsite he saw that the others were asleep. It was just as well, he told himself. He didn't want whispered conversations. The wrong person could wake and draw the right conclusions.

He unsaddled the horse and stayed at the outskirts of the area, setting his bedroll between two junipers. He lay down, and stretched his tired muscles. But he felt good. He had something to go on. He'd get some answers for a change. He let sleep come to him and the night drifted on, perhaps for another hour, maybe two, he wasn't sure, when the scream woke him. It came again, Joanna's voice, from the other side of the campsite, and then the shots, two sharp sounds, one after the other.

Joanna's voice came again, a cry for help. "Over here, oh, God, over here!" Fargo was strapping on his gunbelt as he raced from between the trees, streaked across the camp, and saw the dark shapes of others sitting up. He caught a glimpse of Glory close beside Nugget, who took a moment longer to sit up. Fargo ran into the thick brush and Joanna's voice called out again, just to his right. He whirled and saw her, enough moon up to cast a pale light. The Colt in his hand, he ran to her. She fell into his arms with a gasped shudder and he saw the man's body on the ground, one arm twisted back, the other flung aside. He saw the two small red stains in the front of his shirt and turned to Joanna. He saw a Remington derringer with ivory grips in her hand. She was staring down at the man on the ground, one hand to her face, her eyes wide.

"What the hell happened?" Fargo asked.

"He came to me, woke me," Joanna said. "He said he had something to tell me but was afraid to talk to me in the middle of camp. I went with him. I thought maybe he knew something about what happened. I'd no idea you were back.''

''Then what?''

''We came here. He pulled a knife and tried to kill me. It's still there in his hand,'' Joanna said. Fargo peered down at the man's right hand and saw the long-bladed skinning knife.

''He came at me,'' Joanna went on. ''I tried to run but he knocked me down and came at me again, started to bring the knife down. I had the derringer in the pocket of my robe. I used it,'' she said, and her fingers dug into Fargo's forearm as the others came up. Gus Harby, clothed only in trousers, stared down at the figure on the ground.

''That's McCooney.'' He frowned.

''He tried to kill me,'' Joanna said, shuddering.

''Jesus, why?'' Harby asked.

''I don't know,'' Joanna said. ''Maybe he was just crazy.''

''It's over,'' Fargo said. ''You can talk more about it in the morning.'' They caught the order in his words and started to move away. Fargo saw Glory's eyes on him. His stare told her to leave and she did, her face set as Nugget followed her. Alone, Fargo turned to Joanna again. ''What did he say to you?'' he asked.

''Nothing. He just brought me here and spun on me with the knife,'' she said. Her eyes hardened as she looked at Fargo. ''Why didn't you tell me you'd come back? I wouldn't have gone with him then,'' she said. ''What'd you find?'' she asked.

''Enough,'' he said, and stepped to the lifeless figure. He picked up the man's right foot, his eyes on the boot, and he saw the chip out of the heel. He let the man's foot drop and stood up, his lips a tight line. "He's the one who cut the cinch," he said grimly. "He's the one who tried to kill Glory."

"And now he tried to kill me," Joanna gasped. "It had to be Kale who planted him."

Fargo frowned for a moment. "Yes, I'd say it sure seems that way. Unless he was some kind of lunatic who hated women." Joanna turned a chiding glance at him. "All right, I'm reaching with that," he conceded. He went through the man's pockets but found nothing. He took Joanna's arm as he walked her back to the campsite.

"I won't be able to sleep much now," she said.

"I'll stay with you. I'll get my things."

"Yes, I'd like that," she said, her voice soft.

"Go through his saddlebag with Harby in the morning. See if you find anything," he told her, and she nodded.

When he returned with his bedroll, she was lying on her blanket. He stretched the bedroll out beside her, lay down, and glimpsed Glory turn her back on him as he settled down. Joanna's arm reached over, her hand folding into his, and it wasn't long before he heard her soft, steady breathing as she fell asleep. He let his thoughts drift a little longer. He had found the bad apple in the barrel and that was gratifying. Yet the strange turn of events disturbed him. What had seemed to become clear was suddenly no longer clear.

When morning came, Harby had some of the men bury McCooney and Joanna went through the man's saddlebag with Harby. Fargo found a moment to take Glory aside and Nugget came with her. "He was the one who tried to kill you," Fargo told her, recounting how he'd found the chipped-heel footprint. When he finished, Glory's face wore a half-glower.

"I know what you're thinking," she muttered.

"Do you?"

"Because he tried to kill her you think this puts us back to square one, back to Kale," she said.

"Doesn't it?"

"Not to me," Glory said truculently.

"I think you just can't admit being wrong."

"It's not a matter of admitting. It's a matter of feeling," she said.

"They were after Evie that night and you yesterday, you insist. Where does Joanna fit in if it wasn't Kale?" he pushed at her.

"Maybe this McCooney had more than one boss. Maybe he was taking money from Kale and somebody else," she flung back, and Fargo found himself considering the reply.

"It's possible but not likely," he said.

"Nothing's likely about this," Glory said. She was right on that, he thought.

"Enough jawing," he said gruffly. "You'll have answers when I find Duncan Kale, not before." He called to her as she started to walk away. "Don't try to rig up some makeshift cinch. Use the cinch from McCooney's saddle."

"I'll see to it," Nugget said, hurrying after Glory. She walked quickly, her slender body swaying, trim rear moving with easy grace. No bouncing to her. He walked to the pinto and saddled the horse as the others in the party prepared to ride. The narrow plain stretched out ahead and the high country held mountain paths that were less steep than they had been below. They made good time going northwest and it was late afternoon when Fargo paused at a stream to let the horses drink and the men refill canteens.

His gaze went out to the terrain ahead of them, the tall forests of Canada balsam, ponderosa pine, and Douglas fir. He pointed to a long trail that wandered across a rolling area between stands of aspen as Joanna came up to him. "I'm going on ahead. The rest of you stay on that trail. Camp when it gets dark. I'll get back to you," he told her.

"Let me know this time?" she said with an edge in her voice.

"You expect a repeat?" He frowned.

"No, but it'd have been different if I'd known you were back last night. I could've been killed. You haven't said you were sorry about that," she said reprovingly.

He put his hand over hers. "I'm sorry. Guess it just never got said," he told her, and her smile was forgiveness. He wheeled the pinto in a half-circle and saw Glory nearby.

"Touching," she remarked as he passed.

"Don't be bitchy," he said, pausing beside her. "You'd feel the same way if it had happened to you."

"Maybe," Glory said. "Only I wouldn't come asking for sympathy." She tossed him a sharp glance and rode on. Smiling at the truth in what she'd said, he turned the pinto up a creviced passage and climbed. He reached higher land, found a long ridge that let him make time as he rode northwest. There was only a little light left in the afternoon, the sun at an angle as it began to descend, when he reined to a halt. His eyes were narrow as he looked into the distance. But he caught the glint of blue, high mountain lakes, some really large.

He couldn't see much further, but the land seemed to slope downward. He'd move a little closer come morning, he decided, and turned the pinto down as dusk began to move in. It was dark when he found the trail below and he halted, strained his ears, and caught the sound of voices. He turned south and found the spot where the group had stopped for the night. Most were just beginning to bed down as he unsaddled the pinto, and he saw Glory watching him. "Find anything?" she asked.

"I'm not sure yet," he said.

"Better report it," Glory said waspishly.

"That sharp tongue's going to get you in trouble someday," he snapped, and strode off angrily. Damn her. She knew how to toss darts. He halted in front of a broad-based aspen where Joanna lay on her blanket. "I'm back," he said.

"You don't have to be so sharp about it." Joanna frowned, and he swore at himself first, then at Glory. "Sorry," he said, dropping down beside her.

"You going to bed down up in the trees again?" she asked.

"Not tonight. I want to get an early start come morning."

She pushed up on one elbow and her lips were on his in the blanket of the black night—lingering, moist, enveloping soft. "So's you don't forget," she said.

"I've a good memory," he answered as she sank back on the blanket, and he rose and hurried away. He put his bedroll at the edge of the small area and fell asleep quickly and was awake when the gray of dawn slid across the mountains. He rose and dressed, his gaze roaming north along the rolling land. He saw that the trail remained, widened in fact, and began to move downward.

Gus Harby approached as Fargo saddled the pinto, and he told the man, "Keep right on this trail, far as it takes you. I'm guessing you'll be able to stay with it most of the day."

"Whatever you say." Harby nodded. Fargo saw Glory sit up as he swung onto the pinto and began to ride from the camp. She flashed a slightly smug, pleased smile at him and he glowered back and sent the pinto up a steep trail.

He returned to the high ridge again and rode forward. The lakes were sparkling now in the morning sun. He rode another ten miles as the land began to move downward, more lakes below and he spotted a long, low valley in the distance. Beyond it he saw the wide blue ribbon of a river that wound its way downward over miles too far away to see. He almost smiled as he turned the horse and made his way down a slope, then another, and finally reached the trail below. He was in advance of the others and was resting against a tree when they rode up, surprise in Joanna's eyes.

"I'd say we're getting close to logging country," Fargo said.

"Duncan Kale?" Joanna exclaimed excitedly.

"Maybe. Can't say that yet. But the terrain is right and the trees are right. We'll move forward till dark. We'll still be safe enough then," he said, and swung onto the Ovaro. He rode only a quarter-mile ahead of the others but he saw the land continuing to slope downward. The big valley was still distant but he'd take no chances, and he ordered a halt when dusk came. Joanna sat beside him as they ate cold beef strips, and he saw Glory, Nugget near her, within earshot.

"What happens tomorrow?" Joanna asked.

"We go maybe another ten miles closer," he said.

"And then?"

"I'll be deciding which way to go," he said, and strode away to get his bedroll. He set it down to one side of the area, undressed to his drawers, and lay still as the others settled into sleep. He was about to close his eyes when he saw the slender form materialize out of the dark and drop to one knee beside him. Glory's gaze moved slowly across the beauty of his muscled near-nakedness, finally came to a rest on his face.

"You've your plans already made," she said, and he let silence form the admission. "I'll go along with whatever you want of me. I just wanted you to know that," she told him.

"Thanks," he said. "For me or for Evie?"

She rose and stepped away, let herself be swallowed up by the darkness. Her voice came back through the night. "For both of you."

Fargo slept, waking only when morning came to bathe the land. Then he rose, saddled up, and led the way toward the distant valley. He drew to a halt when they had gone ten miles and had the others dismount while he took the pinto up a steep passage to a hilltop that let him view the land ahead. He saw the bare swaths of land where only tree stumps covered the ground, and he peered further on and saw more such swaths. Logging land lay directly ahead. All the signs were there—the high lakes and the river that ran alongside the valley, the right timber and the cut-down swaths of land.

He turned and sent the pinto down the steep passage to where the others waited. Joanna's eyes were filled with questions. "A logging operation dead ahead, plenty big enough," he said.

"Duncan Kale," Joanna asked.

"Could be. If it is, I want to make sure I get in," Fargo said.

"Meaning what?" Joanna asked.

"Meaning this is as far as you go. I'd like Harby and his men to go back a few miles, in case someone's out looking around."

"And me?" Joanna queried.

"You'll stay here. I'll get word to you soon as I know," he said. "Glory and Nugget will be coming with me."

"What do you need her for?"

"If it's Kale's operation, he'll have people on guard against a single rider. He knows you hired me. He won't be looking for a family man with his wife, and her pa."

"I suppose it makes sense," Joanna conceded.

"I'll get word back to you," Fargo said.

"Please," she said, the word a command. She stepped back and watched as he rode on, Glory and Nugget following. He was into the trees and out of sight in minutes, moving through the tall Douglas firs that rose up on all sides. Glory came up alongside him with Nugget close behind and they rode through the thick, deep green forest. They had gone about half a mile when he pointed out a swath of cleared land that appeared, then another further to the right. They rode for another quarter-mile before he spoke again to her, not looking at her as he did.

"Kale's operation," he murmured.

"How in hell do you know that?" she threw back with a frown.

"We just passed two riflemen, one on each side of the hills. There's another on the right a dozen yards ahead," Fargo said, and saw Glory peer up into the trees.

"I'll be damned," she breathed after a moment.

"Never saw an ordinary logging operation with armed guards," Fargo commented wryly. "And here's our escort," he added as two rifle-bearing riders came from the trees to block their way.

"State your business," one said, a thin-faced man with a hat pulled low over his forehead.

"Looking for a job. Heard you needed loggers," Fargo said. The man took in Glory first, then Nugget.

"Come with us," he said, and Fargo saw the second rider swing in behind them. The men led the way downward where the trail widened. Fargo nudged Glory as they began to see the huge trees with two lumbermen working on each with their double-bitted axes. Some stood on springboards driven into the trees above the baseline. Below and ahead of them Fargo could see the shacks of the logging village and, at the edge of the structures, the river that ran south. Glory's whispered question came to him as she took in the long wooden V-shaped chutes that ran down the long mountainsides, along with wide paths of cross-ties that bordered where they rode.

"What are all these things?"

"I'll give you the cook's tour later," he said, and she fell silent as the two men brought them to the bottom of the slope. Fargo noted the half-dozen wooden rafts tied to the shoreline of the river. Most of the buildings were bunkhouses, and smoke rose from three open cooking fires. The men halted at a flat-roofed building and dismounted, and Fargo swung from the Ovaro. He took the sack of logging equipment from Nugget's mare as the old miner and Glory dismounted. The thin-faced man had entered the building and now he returned.

"Go on in, the boss'll see you," he said, and Fargo stepped inside carrying the sack, Nugget and Glory beside him. The man who looked at him from across the wood desk hadn't tried to change his appearance in any way. He fitted the description Joanna had given, even to the long sideburns, though he was perhaps a trifle handsomer than she had indicated. Fargo took in the man's build, trim and muscular. He was an inch or so taller than Fargo.

"I'm Duncan Kale. This is my operation," the man said as his gaze swept over the trio that faced him.

"Joe Eyks," Fargo said. "Heard you were looking for loggers. Hope you take family men."

"I can use more loggers and we do have half a dozen family men. They stay in their own section, away from the rest of the camp," Kale said. "Where'd you work before?"

"Washington. Mostly ponderosa and sierra redwoods," Fargo said.

"Well, you ought to be at home here. Usual wages," Kale said. His eyes went to Nugget.

"My wife's pa. He was hoping he could find some pick-up work in the camp," Fargo said.

"I'm a fair cook," Nugget put in.

Kale nodded and motioned for them to follow as he stepped outside and spoke to the thin-faced man. "Take the old-timer to Charlie. Tell him to put him to use around the camp," he said, and turned to Fargo. "There's not much of the day left. Report below in the morning for shape-up," he said.

"We'll walk around some and have a look at your operation," Fargo said.

"Sure." Kale shrugged. "The married men's quarters are at the west end of the camp. There's an extra tent you can use till you set up your own." He turned and stepped back into his quarters. Glory linked her arm with Fargo's as they started to stroll through the logging camp.

"It worked," she whispered. "We're in."

"So far so good," he agreed. Glory pointed to the pathway of logs. "It's called a skid road," he explained.

"Dirt is filled in between the cross-ties and timber is pulled down by ox or horse, sometimes by plain manpower. It's used for bringing logs down where there are no really steep grades."

He paused near one of the long V-shaped log chutes Glory had asked about earlier. She saw that the three, each about fifty yards from the others, ran to the river's edge from high up in the mountains, so high the foliage obscured the tops. "They're called flumes," Fargo said. "They carry logs from the high timber areas. They have a shallow amount of water in them and a log, by the time it hits the bottom and the river, can be traveling ninety miles an hour."

"I'm impressed," Glory said. She steered him halfway up a cleared hillside to point to a large lake higher up with a narrow opening at one end. The lake was almost full with huge logs that were jammed one against the other, all crowding at the opening like so many schoolchildren waiting to rush out.

"See that spill gate across the opening?" Fargo asked, and she nodded. "Logs are floated down to sawmills by rivers like the one alongside the camp. Loggers on rafts using long poles with sharp hooks at one end move the logs downriver. But up here in the high land, the rivers have long stretches of rapids. No loggers on rafts can navigate that water, and the rapids usually narrow and the logs jam up there. So they use the splash."

"The splash?"

"That's what they call the release of the floodwaters when the spill gate is opened. All that water rushes through the opening, carrying the logs with it. It hits the river with tremendous power, carrying the logs with it, sending them with force enough to sweep through the rapids and

121

downriver to the sawmill. Other loggers on rafts are far downriver to take charge later on.''

"God, that must be an awesome sight," Glory said, her eyes on the spill gate and the logs jammed behind it.

"It is. That's why they call it the splash. It's the biggest splash you'll ever see when all that water and all those logs hit the river," Fargo said.

"It kind of gives me the shivers," Glory said as she shuddered and walked down the hill with her arm clinging to Fargo. Dusk was sliding over the camp as they walked to the forward edge where a half-dozen shacks were clustered. He saw three women outside, one hanging wash, another washing clothes in a bucket, and a third tossing away slops. One woman was definitely half-Indian, the other two, both in their late thirties, he guessed, had prematurely gray hair. Their glances at Glory were acknowledgment more than welcome. The tent was at the end of the two shacks, a few dozen feet on, and Glory entered it in the last light of the day. It was large enough for three people, and two candles in hollowed-out stones were placed in the center.

"I'll bring our things from the horses," Fargo said. He made two trips, one with the saddle, the second with his bedroll and Glory's pack. She had gotten one of the candles lighted and it gave off a dim, flickering glow.

"What now?" she asked as she began to set out her things.

"Tomorrow I look around some more while I make believe I'm a logger. I've got to figure out the best way to get Kale out of here," Fargo said.

"And into Joanna's hands."

"That'll be better than a shootout with maybe innocent people getting killed," Fargo said. "He's really the only one she wants. I'd like to find out about Burt Dimmons, though."

"You awake in there?" a voice interrupted, and Fargo pulled the tent flap back to see Nugget.

"Come in. They find a job for you?" Fargo asked.

"Helping the cook, pots and pans, cleanup, that kind of thing. But I've been asking questions. The cook's a gabby old bird," Nugget said. "First off, Kale has six armed guards. The rest here are just loggers. I asked cookie why the armed guards and he said that Kale told them he doesn't like visitors."

Fargo smiled. "Good enough answer."

"But he brings the guards in at night and stations them around his quarters," Nugget said. "Come dawn, he sends them out again."

"Interesting." Fargo frowned. "I suppose he figures they couldn't spot somebody sneaking through the trees at night and he wants them protecting his hide by night. This helps."

"Why?" Glory asked.

"It means I can sneak out and get to Joanna when I'm ready. I know she's going to be waiting to hear from me," Fargo answered.

"Heard something about Burt Dimmons, too," Nugget said. "He's the foreman of the operation. You'll see him at the shape-up tomorrow. But at the end of the day, he goes off to the high land at the top of the flumes and spends the night there."

"Why?" Fargo questioned.

"That's what I asked. Nobody seems to know," Nugget said. "But every morning when Kale wakes up, he runs a red flag up a pole alongside his cabin. Nobody seems to know why he does that, either."

Fargo's mind raced and his smile formed slowly. "Because he's one real smart son of a bitch, that's why," Fargo said. "He's arranged it so if someone slips through and gets to him, Dimmons will be alive and able to come save him. The red flag is a signal. Dimmons can see it from high up where he is. If he doesn't see it go up, he knows something's wrong."

"I'll be damned," Nugget said.

"Which means I have to get to Dimmons first," Fargo thought aloud, his lips tightening. "That means tomorrow night. While I'm doing that, you can go to where we left Joanna. Can you do that?"

"I can. I'll find my way, count on it," Nugget said.

"Tell her Kale's here but she's to stay put until I get to her. That's the most important thing. She stays there till I get to her."

"Got it," Nugget said. "Maybe we can talk tomorrow night when I get back."

Fargo nodded and Nugget pushed his way from the tent, his footsteps fading away outside.

"This complicates things," Glory said.

"Maybe, but maybe not all that much. We'll see," he said as he put down his bedroll.

"What do I do tomorrow while you're out making believe you're a logger?" Glory asked.

"Go outside, wash some things, talk to some of the other women. You're supposed to be my wife, remember. Maybe I should give you a shirt to sew," he said.

"That won't be necessary," she said huffily. Fargo sat down, pulled off his boots, and started to undo his shirt. "You're not going outside while I change?" she asked.

He shot her a pained glance. "I can't. What husband goes outside while his wife undresses? What if one of

124

Kale's men is watching? That could mess up the whole thing. We have to keep up appearances,'' he said as he pulled off his shirt.

''And you'd use any excuse,'' she said reprovingly.

''Excuses are meant to be used.'' Fargo smiled affably.

She gazed back at him for a long moment. ''Yes, I suppose they are,'' she said and, without turning, flicked the buttons of her blouse open. Fargo felt a furrow of surprise slide across his brow as she shrugged her shoulders and the blouse fell away entirely. She took a step toward him as he gazed at breasts that, though still modest, were excitingly saucy naked, cups pushing up pertly, each tipped by a delicate pink nipple on an equally delicate areola. She had nicely rounded shoulders and a small ribcage below the pert breasts. She undid her skirt, pushed it down with her underthings, and stood totally naked before him.

He took in her slender loveliness—narrow hips, long beautifully formed thighs, a flat abdomen, and under it a small V. She took another step forward and her arms slid around his neck, the pert breasts pressing into his chest, warm little points. He felt himself responding at once. Her lips pressed his, demanding, and he lowered himself to the bedroll with her. He felt her hands helping him slide away clothes and then he was naked against her and felt the hotness of her skin.

He lay over her, her mouth opened for his, her tongue making quick, darting little motions that increased as his hands covered her breasts, cupped their rounded bottoms, and caressed the delicate pink tips. ''Yes, oh, yes,'' Glory murmured, and pushed her breasts upward. He brought his lips down and gently drew one soft mound into his mouth. His tongue circled, caressed, sucked, and Glory's gasps and groans were sounds of pure pleasure. "Yes, oh, God, yes, yes, . . . ummmmmm . . . yes," she murmured. Her hands slid up and down his chest, along his ribs, dug into his groin. He transferred his mouth to the other breasts and Glory shuddered with pleasure. His hand traced a slow path down her slenderness, felt her ribs, barely covered with flesh. He brought his hand across the flat abdomen and followed the path with his lips.

"Oh, yes . . . oh, good, good . . . oh, good," she breathed as his tongue circled the tiny little indentation in her flat belly, moved downward across the small crest of her pubic mound, the wiry-soft nap pressing into her face. His hand came down to press into her thighs, felt the moistness of her skin, signals of the flesh. He slid his hand upward along the smoothness and her thighs trembled first, then came down slightly. He continued to slide fingers upward slowly but firmly and felt the excitement pulling at him, his own self throbbing, wanting. Glory's skin was moistly smooth, her body pliant, more than willing, a kind of suddenly released energy in her, and he felt the tiny tremors running through her.

His fingers reached, touched more than the moistness of her thighs now, and her legs fell apart as she gave a sudden half-scream. "Oh, God, oh, God, yes, yes . . . yes," Glory cried out, and her pelvis thrust forward, slamming into his hand. He entered, caressed, and she screamed against his chest as her legs kicked out, drew back, and kicked out again. "Please, please, God, please," she cried out against him as he touched the flowing wetness of her darkness, felt her carrying him along with the wild wanting that swept through her. He lifted himself, came atop her, and slid forward, his own pulsatsing warmth touching, thrusting deep, and Glory screamed in pure ecstasy. Her lovely slender thighs closed around him, pressed their moistness against his sides. She began to rock back and forth with him, an erotic cradle of sweeping pleasure. She made little half-moaning sounds as she moved and he reveled in the feel of her around him, the exciting, stimulating, surging, soft caresses of the Venus lips, each one stronger than the one before.

"Oh, oh, my God, oh, yes . . . oh, yes," he heard her suddenly cry out, her voice seized by almost desperate desire, her thighs around him trembling as they tightened. Glory's slim body rose, her pelvis almost leaping upward, the pert breasts jiggling from side to side. "Now, now, now, noooooooowww," she screamed, and he felt himself carried along with her, exploding with her, the world made of sweet, succulent spasms. Her hands, little fists now, pounded against him until her ecstatic cry rose up to hang in midair and slide away. But she still clung to him, her moist, warm body pressed into his, as though she wanted flesh to imprint ecstasy into her.

But finally her thighs grew limp around him and she lifted one arm to wipe away the line of perspiration across her forehead. "My God," she murmured as she grew still, but her arms held him into her a little longer until finally they, too, fell away. He lay beside her, his hand cupping an upthrust breast, with more leisure now to appreciate her slender loveliness. She looked at him with smiling eyes.

"Now, that's what I call keeping up appearances," he commented.

"It was what you said," she answered, pushing up on an elbow, one breast dipping to brush his chest. "About excuses being meant to be used. I didn't realize it till then. I'd been waiting for an excuse, maybe ever since that first day.'' She lay down in his arms, still moist and warm. ''Think we'll have to keep up appearances again tomorrow night?'' she asked.

''Can't say,'' he answered, smiling.

''No matter,'' she murmured. ''I don't need any more excuses.''

He felt her fall asleep against him and he smiled again. He didn't need any excuses, either. He just needed to stay alive.

7

He rose in the morning, borrowed a bucket lying on the ground outside the tent, and went down to the river to fill it with cool water. When he came back, Glory was sitting up and looking deliciously lovely, round little breasts turned upward invitingly. He let the cold water stifle the stirrings that immediately swept through him, and she waited till he finished washing and watched him pull on clothes. She sat on the bedroll, arms stiff, resting on the palms of her hands. "Damn you, you're doing that on purpose," he growled. Her little smug smile was admission. He grunted as he picked up the sack.

" 'Bye, husband," she said as he stepped to the tent flap, laughter in her voice. He hurried out, not daring to look back at her again. He strode to where the men were gathered in a half-circle, facing a stocky, powerfully built man. Oxlike, Joanna had said of Dimmons, and the description fit, right to the receding hairline and the small scar on the man's upper lips. Burt Dimmons paused as Fargo came to a halt to stand beside the others.

"You're the new man," he said. "What equipment did you bring with you?"

"A bucking saw, my lubricant cans, and a falling ax," Fargo said.

"Forget the ax for now," Dimmons said, and pointed to a smallish man with a wiry build. "Take your saw and go with Harry, there. You can start cutting up downed timber."

"Yes, sir," Fargo said.

"And leave your gunbelt with the cook. We don't allow guns in camp. We don't want arguments to end in gunfights," Dimmons said. "Besides, it's for your safety. I've seen loggers fall wearing guns and get shot with their own gun."

Fargo nodded and joined the smallish man. He paused at the cook's wagon, where he saw Nugget cleaning pans. Fargo handed the cook his Colt.

"You can stop by and pick it up whenever you decide to leave camp," the cook said.

Fargo followed the wiry man to the side of the mountain where long trees lay stretched out in parallel rows. The long bucking saw was designed for two men to use, and he and Harry began at the base end of one of the downed trees. Fargo was surprised at how quickly thick pitch gathered on the saw blade and how often he had to resort to the lubricant can.

By midday his shoulders ached from the unaccustomed motions, but by the time the afternoon ended his muscles had grown more accustomed to the work. As dusk began to descend he returned to the tent. Glory had made a small fire just outside and he saw strips of dried beef heated over the flame.

"How'd it go, logger?" she asked as he sat down and stretched his arm muscles.

"It's not a career I want to take up," he said as she handed him a stick with a strip of beef on it. "Tonight I'm going up to visit Burt Dimmons."

"Visit? What's that really mean?"

"I don't know. Evie came to me to ask that I try and see he's not hurt or killed. I'd like to do that for her," Fargo said.

"That'd be good," Glory agreed.

"But I can't leave him to come after us when I get Kale," Fargo said. "It's going to be sticky. I'll do the best I can. Can't promise more than that."

"Evie wouldn't ask more than that," Glory said softly. They finished the meal in silence. She doused the little fire with a tin of water and went into the tent, and he followed her. She was holding fast to him at once. "Be careful. Last night was too wonderful to have it be a one-time thing," she said.

"I couldn't agree more," he told her. Just then Nugget poked his head into the tent.

"Sorry," the old miner muttered. "You're doing this husband-and-wife thing up real well, it seems."

"It seems," Glory said.

"You find Joanna last night?" Fargo asked.

"Yes. She got real excited when I told her it was Kale's operation," Nugget told Fargo. "She said she'd wait to hear from you. Harby and the rest of the men were still there. She hadn't moved them back."

"That's just cussedness on her part," Fargo said. "I'll get to her when I'm through with Dimmons. I hope," he added grimly.

"I'll look for you in the morning," Nugget said as he left with a nod to Glory. Fargo lay down with her, held her until the sprawling camp began to settle into sleep. He rose then, left with the taste of her mouth on his, and paused to survey the towering mountain forests illuminated by an almost full moon. He chose the flume at the very end of the mountainside and began to climb alongside its V-shaped wooden sides. The climb was longer than he'd expected, the side of the mountain higher and steeper than it appeared. But he finally reached the top, rested on one knee for a moment, and then began to move across a flat area. He could see the towering redwoods that rose up just in back of the flumes, proud sacrifices that would one day careen down the mile-a-minute chutes.

He spied the shack, obviously hastily built, resting between two of the flumes, a lamplight in its lone window. He approached the door and wished the Colt was strapped to his hip, certain that Burt Dimmons would have a firearm somewhere close. He'd thought about what he'd say and had come up with nothing that satisfied him. He'd play it by ear, he'd decided, and hope for the best. He knocked, heard the man stir inside the shack, and then the door opened and he faced Burt Dimmons's frowning face.

Dimmons stared at him. "You're the new man. What the hell are you doing up here?"

"Evie wanted me to talk to you," Fargo said.

Burt Dimmons came outside instantly, his frown deepening. "Evie? What do you know about Evie?"

"She told me about you," Fargo said.

Dimmons halted, his face all suspicion as he peered hard at the big man in front of him. "You're not a logger," he said after a moment. "You're him, the one Joanna Petersen hired. You slipped your way in." Dimmons took another step forward, his every motion threatening now, tension suffusing his body. "What about Evie? What do you know about Evie?" he demanded.

"Evie's dead," Fargo said, and saw the shock smash through Dimmon's face. The shock turned into darkening disbelief.

"Evie dead? You goddamn bastard, Evie dead?" he bellowed.

"I'll explain. You don't understand," Fargo said, but the man's face only grew more livid and his lips twitched.

"I understand, you fucking bastard. You made her tell you where we went and then killed her," Dimmons roared.

"No, that's not the way it was," Fargo said.

"Goddamn bastards!" Dimmons screamed. "Goddamn you!" He flung his oxlike body forward with the force of a buffalo's charge. Fargo started to whirl aside, but Burt Dimmons bowled into him and he felt himself go backward and down. He hit the ground on his back as the man's curses rang in his ears. "You're dead, you stinkin' bastard, dead!" Dimmons roared. He came down with both hands outstretched for Fargo's throat. Fargo managed to get a forearm up that sent the man off-balance. "Kill you, I'll kill you!" Dimmons screamed, but Fargo had seized the moment and whirled sideways. He rolled and felt the man's blow barely miss the back of his head.

Fargo sprang to his feet as Dimmons charged again. He wanted to say something to halt the man, but Dimmons was berserk in the grip of a towering rage, completely beyond reason. Fargo sidestepped and sent a whistling blow into the man's midsection that would have doubled up most opponents. Dimmons only grunted and swung a treelike arm sideways that caught Fargo across the side of his neck. Fargo felt his breath vanish for an instant and pain shoot up his head as he staggered sideways. Dimmons was at him again, slamming into him with ramrod force. Fargo felt himself falling, twirling, hitting the ground. Dimmons was an insane man, his face contorted with rage as he started to dive forward again. "She was good, a good person, you son of a bitch," Dimmons snarled. Fargo used the power in his calves to twist his body sideways just enough so the pile-driver blow slammed into the ground.

Fargo swung around again, regaining his feet as Burt Dimmons came in with his head lowered, both powerful arms swinging looping blows. Fargo dodged one, then another, stepped forward to deliver a crisp left hook. The blow bounced off the man's jaw, hardly slowing him, and Fargo had to duck another looping left followed by a sweeping right. Fargo backtracked, aware that the numbing pain in the side of his neck was fading, his strength starting to return. But Dimmons was a wild man who had only one thought in his crazed mind. He charged again and Fargo sidestepped, threw a left that only slowed the powerful form. Dimmons spun, surprisingly quick, flung a sideways swiping blow that crashed into Fargo's ribs. Fargo winced in pain but he easily avoided the follow-up blow and started to step to his left. His foot hit a piece of log and he heard himself curse as he went down face first over the log. He glimpsed the high wood side of one of the flumes directly behind him as he rose to one knee.

Burt Dimmons was attacking again, but this time Fargo didn't try to get up to meet the bull-like charge. He stayed down, tightened the muscles of his thighs, and half rose as though he were starting to get up, and Dimmons flung himself forward. But Fargo dropped down again and

Dimmons passed over him instead of slamming into him with the force of his oxlike strength. As Dimmons came over him Fargo rose, pushing up with all the strength of his legs. He caught the man's hurtling body from below, flung it upward with all his strength as he would a sack of grain. He saw Burt Dimmons go up in a half-flip, the small of his back slamming against the edge of the flume. Dimmons's legs went upward and the man disappeared over the edge of the flume. Fargo leaped to his feet as he heard Dimmons scream, surprise in his voice for an instant and then bloodcurdling fear.

Fargo grasped the edge of the flume, reached out to try to grasp Burt Dimmons but saw the man's body already rushing down the V-shaped funnel on the shallow bed of water. He saw Dimmons strike against one side, then the other, still screaming, and he heard the scream begin to trail away as Dimmons's body gathered speed. There'd be no place he could grasp onto along the smooth sides of the flume. By now Dimmons was already traveling fifty miles an hour. His body would be going close to eighty or ninety when he reached the bottom of the flume, and he was probably dead already. Fargo grimaced as he crossed the ridge of land and began to climb down the steep side at the opposite end of the ridge.

It hadn't turned out at all as he'd wanted, and when he reached the tent there was pain in the words he flung at Glory. "Dimmons is dead. He never gave me a chance to explain anything. He went crazy when I told him Evie was dead, stark, raging mad."

"Don't blame yourself. You couldn't have known he'd react that way," Glory said.

"I'm not blaming myself. He'd have killed me if I hadn't

fought back. I'd no choice. I'm just sorry it turned out the way it did. I wanted to keep my word to Evie. He never gave me the chance,'' Fargo said.

Glory offered a rueful smile, sadness in her eyes. "In his own way, I guess he cared just as deeply as she did," Glory murmured. "Both of them lost souls, each in their own way."

Fargo frowned. "I'm sure of one thing. If Kale sent the men who killed Evie he never told Burt Dimmons he was doing it."

"You saying more than that?" Glory asked.

"Nope," he said. "Just that. I'm going to Joanna. I want to make sure she doesn't do anything stupid." He took a moment to return Glory's kiss and then hurried from the tent. Moving in a crouch, he circled behind the cook's shack and wagon, saw the two armed guards outside Kale's hut, and circled to lead the Ovaro from where the horses were tethered in a group. Deciding not to risk the time or the noise to put on saddle and bridle, he swung onto the horse and rode bareback into the heavy forest land.

The almost full moon filtered enough light down for him to make good time, and he rode into the small clearing where he'd left Joanna in a noisy canter. He glimpsed the movement along the far trees, men waking and pushing to their feet, and he stayed in the open as he swung from the horse. Joanna appeared, the blue robe wrapped around her, hurrying toward him. "Where's Duncan?" she asked abruptly and sharply.

"In the camp. His place is right in the center," Fargo told her. "I'll make my move tomorrow night."

"You'll bring him here," Joanna said, and he nodded.

"That's what you want, isn't it? You want to question

him, find out where he has the rest of the money he stole,'' Fargo said.

"Yes, but I want you to leave that strictly to me. I know how to handle Duncan Kale," Joanna said emphatically.

"I'm just here to deliver the goods," Fargo said.

"What about Burt Dimmons?" Joanna asked.

"He's dead," Fargo told her. "I never got the chance to talk to him."

"No matter. He didn't count," Joanna said. She stared into space for a moment, her eyes speculative. She brought her gaze back to Fargo after a moment. "Any chance of your getting to Duncan before tomorrow night?" she asked.

"No," he said. "The place is too busy, too much going on." She thought over his reply briefly and then nodded. Fargo climbed back onto the Ovaro and cast a glance across the small clearing. "Why didn't you send the men back as I told you to do?" he asked her.

"I decided I didn't want to stay here alone. I wanted some protection."

"You could've ruined everything. If any of Kale's guards had come out this far and seen them they'd have known there was trouble," Fargo chastised.

"They didn't and it doesn't matter now," Joanna said brusquely. Fargo shrugged and sent the Ovaro from the small clearing. He rode back without hurrying, dismounted when he neared the logging camp, and walked the horse in a circle to return him to where the other horses were grouped. He carefully made his way back to the tent, pausing to note that the two guards in front of Kale's quarters were asleep on their feet as they leaned against the building. The moon was almost all the way across the sky as he slipped into the tent.

Glory woke at once and he shed clothes and lay down beside her. She pressed her warm body tight against him with a sigh of contentment and they fell asleep. He woke with the yellow light of the morning sun against the tent. Glory had filled the water bucket and he washed and dressed, then sat back and enjoyed watching her unstudied grace as she moved about the tent. "We'll make plans for tonight when the day's finished," he told her as she curled her hand in his to leave the tent with him.

He stepped outside and came to a halt. Duncan Kale waited outside the tent, two of his rifle-carrying guards flanking him. "That's as far as you go," Kale said, his voice hard. Fargo let go of Glory's hand and she stepped away from him. "Who are you, mister?" Kale growled.

"Joe Eyks," Fargo said. "What's this all about?"

"We found Burt Dimmons's body," Kale said. "At the bottom of the flume, half in the river."

Fargo kept his face impassive as thoughts raced through his mind. He cursed silently. The thousand-pound timbers hit the bottom of the flumes and plowed into the river with all the force of weight and momentum behind them. Burt Dimmons's body had only the momentum. It had just splattered onto the shoreline. "What's that got to do with me?" Fargo asked. "Why come looking for me?"

"Everything's been peaceful around here. You show up and Burt's found dead," Duncan Kale said. "You're going to talk. Your little wifey, too, if that's what she is." He motioned to the two guards. "Bring them both," he said. Fargo's eyes flicked to the rest of the camp area. The loggers were preparing to go to work. They weren't watching, except for a few casual glances. He saw one guard take Glory by the arm while the second one approached him, rifle held in both hands diagonally in front of him.

"Let's go," the man said, halting in front of him. Fargo shrugged disconsolately and then, with the speed of a cougar's slash, he brought both hands up, seized the rifle by the base of the stock and the barrel, and twisted as he slammed into the man. The rifle pulled free in his hands as the man went stumbling backward, but Fargo was whirling, firing, more for effect than accuracy. He saw Kale fling himself flat on the ground, and the man holding Glory pulled her down with him.

Out of the corner of his eye Fargo saw other men with rifles running toward him and he whirled, started to race away. The guard he'd knocked down came up pulling a pistol from his belt. Fargo fired the rifle as he ran past and the man made shuddering motions as he flew backward, a shower of red spraying from him. Fargo ran, mustering all the power of his legs, and heard two shots miss him as he reached the trees and ran onto the forest land. He turned, ran up a slope thickly covered with sierra redwoods. He changed direction, ran deeper into the thickness of the forest. He could hear his pursuers chasing after him but losing ground fast. He turned again and paused, his eyes sweeping the deep green of low-branched thickets. He ran higher and saw the mountainside become ridged with the huge tree trunks all but obscuring the indentations in the soil.

He found one long, narrow gouge and crawled into it, made his way along it to where a dense growth of thick mountain scrub rose up to completely obscure the horizontal crevice. He lay motionless, listening, and his ears traced the paths of the searchers. Others had come up to scour the forest and he heard Duncan Kale's voice shouting orders. The searchers pushed their way through brush, thereby losing any signs of footprints there might have been, and with true amateurness, erased any they might have missed. Finally the sound of their aimless searching came to an end and he heard them trudging their way down the mountainside.

Fargo didn't move. Kale was smart and extremely canny. He might have left a few men behind. There was no need to take the risk. He knew what Kale would do. The man would hold Glory and wait for a rescue attempt to be made. Glory would tell him that she was part of the scheme to get into the camp. There'd be no point in denying it and no gain in being roughed up for something Kale had already concluded. But Glory had a sharp mind. She'd say nothing about Joanna being but a few miles away.

Right now Kale was still convinced that he held the high cards. He had Glory, and the man sent to get him was hiding in the mountains. He had essentially broken up the attempt to kill him. All he had to do now was wait to finish the job. He'd have his guards strategically placed to cover every approach to the shack. Maybe he had Nugget also, Fargo considered, and his thoughts continued to reflect Duncan Kale's evaluation. If Glory was abandoned, no attempt made to save her, he'd simply kill her, aware that the man sent to get him fled. He'd win, either way.

Fargo grunted bitterly. Kale had good reason to feel he held the high cards. Fargo pushed backward a few feet, settled into the hiding place to let the hours pass. When the sun moved into the afternoon sky, he crawled from the slitted hideaway and moved carefully down the mountainside, pausing every dozen yards to listen. But he heard only the forest sounds and he continued his careful trek downward. He halted, still on the mountain fastness as night descended, and he waited till the moon rose. He let the hours go by, waiting till the camp had settled into sleep, before he continued down. The dark outlines of the buildings finally came into view, moonlight picking up the strewn timbers half cut and the darkened bunkhouses, and he rested on one knee for a moment to pick out Kale's hut.

A lamp burned low inside and his gaze traveled around the edges of the area near the hut. He picked out the crouching figures, some behind logs, others against tool shacks, each with a rifle in hand. They were waiting for someone to approach Kale's hut, ready to send a fusillade of bullets through the night. Fargo backed silently away, circled, and moved along the low trees where the horses were grouped. He halted, and again his eyes swept the perimeter of the area. He grimaced as he spied the first dark outline, then the second and then a third. Duncan Kale left no loose ends. He knew that even if Glory was to be abandoned, a man would need a horse to flee these rugged mountains. Again Fargo backed away, returning to a spot behind a small pyramid of cut timber that let him look out at Kale's hut.

The man had Glory inside, of course, but to try to get to her now would be to commit suicide. He'd have to wait, watch, and bide his time, Fargo realized. Maybe they'd change guards. Maybe a chance would take shape. He might even have to wait for dawn. Kale would surely send some of his men back into the forest to take up their guard posts. With a smaller number of guards around the hut, maybe the hustle and bustle of the logging camp could afford enough cover for him to reach the hut. The world was suddenly filled with maybes, he realized, but he had no options otherwise. He was settling down, his gaze idly moving back into the deep dark of the trees, when suddenly he saw the movement, shadow on shadow.

He sat up, peering into the dark. The movement came again. It seemed to be an arm waving from side to side.

Fargo's glance went to the guards behind him watching Kale's hut. Their concentration remained fixed and he began to crawl across the ground toward the trees. The movement came again and he was almost there when he saw the moonlight pick up a patch of thick hair, now a gray-silver sheen. Fargo reached the trees, his voice a whisper of surprise. "Jesus, I thought they had you, too," he said.

"I was watching from behind the cook's wagon when they came for you this morning. I saw you get away and I disappeared," Nugget said. "They looked for me some, but they mostly concentrated on you. I hid out and crawled back here tonight. I figured this is where you'd come. But I couldn't get your eye until now." Nugget paused and his gaze went across the dark of Kale's hut. "You have any ideas how to get her?" he asked.

"No," Fargo said. "But I know one thing. I want to save her and I don't want Kale to get away."

"You figure you can do both?" Nugget asked.

"Not alone, but I've been thinking about the man. He won't try to run the ordinary way," Fargo said. "He's too smart."

"Such as taking his horse and hightailing it," Nugget said.

"That's right. First, he'd be afraid I'd follow if I were around, and probably catch him. He'd go the fastest way, downriver by raft," Fargo said. "That's where you come in." Nugget frowned the question. "You've seen that spill gate at the edge of the high lake, with all the logs jammed up behind it, haven't you?"

"Yes."

"I want you to climb up there. You can start soon as we finish here," Fargo said. "Come morning, you'll be up there by the spill gate. You'll be able to see the whole damn site from up there. Everything's going to look damn small to you, but you'll be able to see it."

"And then?"

"You see one raft leave the shore and head downriver, you open that spill gate," Fargo said. "Maybe you'll see more than one. Maybe all his men will try to run by raft downriver. No matter. All you have to do is see one raft set out and you open that spill gate."

"You're betting Kale will be on that raft," Nugget said.

Fargo nodded. "Alone or maybe with some of his men. You won't be able to tell that from way up there. You just let those logs go."

"And you?"

Fargo's smile was grim. "I'll have Glory. If I don't, it'll be over for both of us. Either way, Kale won't get away."

"What about Joanna?"

"There's no time to try and get to her. I'll tell her what happened afterwards," Fargo said. "Or you will," he added. The three words needed no explaining.

"Good luck," Nugget said, and he moved backward into the trees and was gone in seconds. Fargo crouched down and began to crawl back to the pyramid of lumber to take up his vigil again. The hours brought not only impatience but a growing despair. The guards did not change shifts. No opportunities presented themselves and the moon had slid to the end of the sky. He continued to keep his silent vigil as the night ended and he saw the first gray light of dawn creep over the tops of the towering redwoods on the high mountains.

He began to slide backward toward the forest line. In a few minutes his pyramid of lumber would no longer be a hiding place. The night had passed and he'd found no way to reach Glory. But nothing had happened to put her in more danger than she was now. He was trying to be sanguine about that small favor as he reached the forest line when the stillness suddenly erupted. The crashing of horses at a gallop through the brush came first, and split seconds later Gus Harby and his men charged into the open from three directions, unloosing a hail of gunfire as they came.

Fargo saw Kale's guards whirl, surprised and confused for an instant, then bring their rifles up to return fire. But three were cut down in the first volley from Harby's men and Fargo saw loggers coming out of the bunkhouses, struggling into trousers as they did. He saw six of them go down. Harby and his men were firing with total indiscrimination. Fargo's glance went to the edge of the trees to see Joanna poised there on the big bay. Three more of Kale's men fired from in front of the hut, brought down two of Harby's attackers, and then scattered and ran to avoid return fire.

But Fargo glimpsed the figure racing around the back corner of the hut, dragging Glory along, and he rose and began to streak forward. "Shit!" he cursed, running zigzag fashion to avoid the bullets plowing into the ground all around him. He saw three more loggers fall as they tried to get back to bunkhouses. Harby's men were firing at anything that moved. They'd probably been given orders to do just that.

Still cursing, racing in a half-crouch, Fargo rounded the rear of the hut and saw Kale, half carrying, half dragging Glory with him, making for the river. Digging deeper into the ground, Fargo summoned another burst of speed and Kale half turned just in time to see the figure diving at him.

8

Fargo slammed into Duncan Kale and the man went sprawling. But most important was that Glory was knocked from his grasp. Kale turned and started to rise and Fargo's kick caught him alongside the temple and he went down again. Racing past him, Fargo yanked Glory to her feet. Wild bullets were still zinging through the site and, one arm around her, Fargo ran toward the tent on the slope. He reached it and glanced back to see Joanna, on her horse, come around the corner of the hut with Gus Harby and another of his men on foot. She pointed to Duncan Kale as the man struggled to his feet, and Harby took command of him.

Joanna barked orders Fargo couldn't hear, but he watched from the tent flap as Duncan Kale was taken back inside the hut and Joanna dismounted and followed him in. Fargo stepped back inside the tent and Glory clung to him. "Kale told me you were dead," she said.

"That's been rumored before," Fargo said. "Nugget's alive, too."

She gave a little squeal of relief. "Where is he?" she asked.

"On assignment," Fargo said, and drew a frown. When he didn't explain further, Glory shrugged and stepped back.

"It's over. Joanna won," she said.

"She damn near got your head blown off with that damn-fool stunt," Fargo snapped. "Kale could've put a bullet through you."

Glory shrugged again. "Guess I was lucky he decided to take me as a hostage," she said. "Shouldn't we go down to Joanna?"

"You stay here. I'll go down. I don't like what's happened. Something stinks. I want to find out why she deliberately disobeyed my orders to stay put," Fargo said. Glory nodded and followed the nod with a kiss that lingered as he walked down the hill. Slain bodies were being picked up, some by Harby's men, more by loggers. Other lumberjacks were gathered in small clusters and an air of stunned confusion and fear hung over the camp. Fargo felt his anger at Joanna growing. He reached the hut, walked around it to the front door, and saw Gus Harby standing there.

"You can't go in," the man said, and Fargo's frown was instant.

"The hell I can't," he growled.

"Miss Petersen's orders," Harby said.

"This some kind of damn joke?"

"She said to keep you outside if you showed up," Harby said, and there was apology in his voice. Harby wasn't a really bad sort, Fargo knew. He'd been hired and his loyalties lay with his paycheck. But he was neither terribly quick nor terribly bright, and he relied on the threat of the gun at his hip more than was wise. A major mistake, Fargo reflected silently as he faced Gus Harby, his arms dangling loosely. Suddenly his right fist shot out. The straight blow sank into Harby's gut with pile-driver force. Harby grunted as he doubled over and Fargo brought the side of his hand down across the back of the man's neck.

Harby pitched forward and lay still at his feet, and Fargo reached down and lifted the gun from its holster. He emptied the bullets from it and flung them away. He didn't want shots that might trigger more wildness. He dropped the gun on the ground as he pushed his way into the hut. Duncan Kale sat behind a small wood desk in the single room and Joanna, standing, faced him with a Smith & Wesson five-shot, single-action piece in her hand. Her eyes widened in surprise as Fargo stepped in.

"Why?" Fargo bit out at her, his eyes cold as ice floes.

Joanna's face covered her surprise quickly. "Why what?"

"You damn well know what. Why'd you try to keep me out and why'd you come barging in against my orders?"

"It was time," Joanna said.

"Just like that?" Fargo frowned.

"Just like that," she repeated. "You're not needed here now. Your part's finished." He heard the ice in her voice and flashed a glance at Kale. A wry smile flickered on Kale's lips.

"That means she's finished using you," Kale said.

"Shut up, Duncan!" Joanna shouted furiously.

Fargo's eyes stayed on Joanna. "Why'd you set off this bloodbath? Why didn't you wait for me to bring him to you?"

Duncan Kale's voice cut in. "She was afraid I might tell you things," he said.

"Shut up, damn you, Duncan!" Joanna screamed at him.

"What kind of things?" Fargo pressed.

"Things that don't concern you, Fargo," Joanna shot back. "Now, get out, out."

Duncan Kale's voice came again. The man's handsome face wore a bitterly sardonic smile. "Tell him, Joanna. No need to hold back anything now. You've won," he said.

"I warned you, Duncan," she said, raising the revolver, and Fargo heard her voice break. She was nearly out of control.

"Hold back what?" he questioned, keeping his own voice calm.

Joanna swung the gun at him. "Get out, for the last time," she hissed, her eyes blazing fury.

"She helped me steal every penny I took from her father," Kale said. "I couldn't have done it without her. He trusted the books to her."

Fargo felt the surprise spiral inside him. "Is that true?" he asked Joanna.

Kale answered again for her. "Of course it's true. She hated the old man, hated everything about him. She was happy to help me. Besides, we were secret lovers," he said.

Fargo frowned at the despairing cry in Joanna's voice as she turned to Kale. "Yes, I loved you, damn you. I loved you. I believed all those promises about our running off together."

"I was thinking about coming back for you," Kale said

quickly. He was shrewd, Fargo saw. It was plain that behind her hate, Joanna still loved.

"No, you weren't. It was a lie, all of it. You were so clever. You used me. You had it all figured out," Joanna flung back at him. "You knew I couldn't tell Father anything. I couldn't even hint at knowing where you might go. I couldn't tell him how you managed to steal the money for so long a time. I could only tell him you'd fooled me. You knew I couldn't say anything or do anything to go after you without implicating myself. You were so damn clever."

Fargo shook his head in amazement at Kale's smile— that of a man modestly accepting a tribute. But suddenly the despair and pain in Joanna's voice vanished, replaced by icy fury.

"But then something happened, something you couldn't have foreseen in a thousand years. The stroke. Father became a vegetable, unable to know anything or understand anything. And I was suddenly free to go after you," Joanna said, and Fargo saw that Duncan Kale's face had lost its sardonic calm. "When word got to you about the stroke you knew I'd come after you. You knew I had to," she went on. "Only you and I knew the truth."

Fargo's brow furrowed as Joanna's words suddenly exploded a rush of thoughts through his mind. "Except for Burt Dimmons," he said. "Burt Dimmons knew the truth."

"Yes, Burt was the only other person who knew," Kale said, but Fargo's eyes were riveted on Joanna.

"And you didn't know what he might have told Evie," Fargo said, thoughts forming as he spoke. "You didn't know and you couldn't take a chance. You couldn't risk her telling me something that might have made me pull out right then and there." Joanna's lips were a thin line as she returned his stare.

"Glory was right all along about that night," he went on. "They were after Evie, not me. Only she never thought about you being the one who sent them. Neither did I." Fargo's eyes narrowed as one thought triggered another in a stampede of realization. "Nobody planted the cowpoke who tried to kill Glory on the cliff trail. You hired him, gave him his instructions. And then you faked that incident in camp. He never came to you. You took him into the woods, shot him, and placed the skinning knife in his hand. I swallowed your story hook, line, and sinker."

"Joanna's a very clever young woman," Duncan Kale said, but Fargo's gaze was still on Joanna and he saw the fury in her face.

"She's a twisted up little bitch," Fargo said.

"And you're a dead man, Fargo. You brought it on yourself. You should've listened to Harby and stayed outside and let me finish with Duncan," Joanna said.

Fargo's gaze dropped to the gun in Joanna's hands. She held it firmly, one finger lightly resting on the trigger. "I guess it's just a question of who you kill first," he said.

"I'm deciding that now," Joanna said, her voice ice. Fargo's eyes went to Duncan Kale. The man hadn't moved in the chair. Fargo tried to send messages with his eyes as he stared at Kale. He flicked a glance at Joanna and back again to the man. He was trying to tell Kale they'd have a chance if they worked together. Make a sudden move, a diversion, his eyes said. She'll spin at you and I'll have a split second to grab her from the side. Duncan

Kale stared back at him and Fargo was certain the man had picked up the message.

But suddenly Kale smiled, a slow, thoughtful smile, and Fargo cursed inwardly as he realized something. Kale had heard the same thing in Joanna's voice that he had. Beneath all her fury, she still loved Kale—a twisted, tormented love perhaps, but it was still there. Kale was going to take his chances on that. He was going to let her kill Fargo and then try to work his own brand of magic. A flame that was still there could be rekindled.

"You bastard," Fargo said quietly.

Kale continued to smile. "A man has to play his cards," he said.

Joanna, with trigger-fast acuteness, picked up the unsaid at once. "What's going on?" she said sharply. Her eyes went to Kale for a moment and Fargo knew he'd never get another chance. He flung his arm out in a backward blow. It caught Joanna along the side of her face and the gun went off, a shot plowing into the wall of the hut as she stumbled sideways. She tried to whirl and bring the gun around, but Fargo had followed through and now he closed his hand over her wrist and forced her arm backward.

She fired again, two shots that went past him. That made three altogether. Keeping count was important. Fargo twisted away to avoid her knee, which came up aimed at his groin. Kale had dropped when the second two shots exploded, and out of the corner of his eye, Fargo saw Kale, bent over, heading for the door. Joanna brought her other hand up, nails outstretched to claw Fargo's eyes, and he twisted his head away. He spun with her and slammed her against the wall, and the gun went off again.

Four, he muttered inwardly. He kept his fingers closed tightly around her wrist as she tried to twist her arm free. She fought furiously, and he used his other arm to keep off her clawing, scratching hand as he kept twisting his body to avoid her blows to his groin.

"I'll kill you, damn you! I'll kill you!" Joanna cried, and he winced as she drove her foot down on his toes with all the force she could muster. He used his forearm to block another attempt at his eyes, stepped back with her, swung her in a circle and let centrifugal force help him slam her against the wall again. The force of the blow tightened her trigger finger and the gun fired again. Five, Fargo counted. That was all the Smith & Wesson held. He opened his hand, yanked her toward him, and twisted the now-empty gun from her fingers as she fell to one knee. He flung it out the long window of the hut as he spun and raced outside, paused for a moment to let his eyes sweep the camp. Those loggers still left were huddled by the bunkhouses, and he saw the remaining handful of Harby's men to one side, looking on, uncertain what to do. Harby was still unconscious in front of the hut. Fargo's gaze swept the camp to spot Duncan Kale.

The man was racing for one of the rafts pulled up on the shore, half of it floating in the water. Fargo dug his heels into the soil as he started to race after Kale. A sudden scream behind him made him glance back, and he saw Joanna stumble out of the hut. He continued running, her screams carrying after him. Kale was almost at the raft, but he halted when he saw Fargo gaining fast. The man took a step sideways and glanced across the ground, and Fargo saw him bend over and come up with a broadax. Fargo continued to rush at him, but now he let his own gaze sweep the ground and he saw it was strewn with the heavy axes dropped by the lumbermen when the attack erupted. Without slowing his stride, he scooped up a broadax and only slowed when he reached Kale.

The man half circled, the heavy ax poised. He continued to circle and Fargo moved forward, his own ax ready. He tried a blow, almost a feint, to get the feel and balance of the weapon. Kale's handsome face was darkened with hatred now, his eyes glowering slits. Fargo struck with the heavy ax, no feint this time, a sweeping blow. Kale ducked under it and brought his own ax upward with both hands, and Fargo had to twist away as the ax blade whistled past his face. Kale was quick, Fargo realized as he circled. He saw Joanna approach, halting near the two circling figures, and once again Fargo tried a blow, a short, chopping stroke aimed at Kale's shoulder.

The man pulled away and managed to avoid the ax. He countered with his own short jab from the side, which Fargo danced away from. Kale suddenly charged. The man swung the broadax with a long, sweeping stroke, all his strength behind it, and Fargo raised his own weapon to parry the blow. Kale swung the ax again and yet again, and Fargo used the flat, broad side of his ax as a shield. He gave ground, parrying each blow until Kale halted, his breath coming in long gasps. Fargo swung his broadax as Kale had done, with long, sweeping blows, and this time it was Kale who backtracked, able only to parry with his ax.

But suddenly he halted as he parried another blow, and Fargo tried to pull back but he wasn't quick enough. Kale slipped the edge of his blade into the narrow space between the handle and the blade of Fargo's broadax. The blade hooked in, Kale twisted as he pulled, and Fargo felt his own ax yanked from his grip. With a shout of triumph,

Kale flung Fargo's ax away and rushed forward with a sweeping stroke. Fargo knew he'd never avoid it by trying to go backward. He flung himself flat, felt the blade swish over his head, and stuck out one leg to trip Kale up as his momentum carried him forward. He saw Kale go down, cursing, but with a firm grip on his broadax. Fargo leaped to his feet and raced to where his ax had been flung, pounced on the weapon and spun around.

Joanna was almost beside Kale as the man paused. "Get the raft, Joanna," he ordered, and Fargo saw her stare at Kale. "Get it into the water. We'll get out of here, just the two of us," Kale said. "It'll be like you always wanted it to be."

Fargo swore softly as he saw Joanna turn, pick up one of the long loggers' poles with the metal hooked point at one end, and run to the raft. He ran at Kale, his broadax raised, as Joanna used the leverage of the pole to push the raft into the water. She stepped onto the raft and held it at the shoreline as Kale leaped aboard, then began to push away with the pole. Cursing, Fargo stayed at a full run, his ax still raised. The raft was still only a few feet from the shore but Kale had gone to the center, confident they were on their way.

The raft was some six feet from the shore now as Fargo leaped, using every last ounce of strength in his powerful legs. He saw the surprise on Kale's face as the man watched Fargo sail through the air, land at the very edge of the raft, teeter for a moment and then regain his balance. Kale let out a roar of rage as he rushed forward, his broadax raised to swing. Fargo held his ground, measuring vital split seconds, and dropped low as Kale swung. The blow went over his head and he saw Kale twist his body sideways to avoid going off the edge of the raft.

But the man was strong and his body in good shape. He managed to save himself and spun as Fargo moved across the square raft. Fargo saw that Joanna had stopped poling to watch, and Kale barked at her, "Keep poling! Get to the center where the current will take you. I'll see to him." Joanna returned to using the long pole and Fargo watched Kale carefully circle. Joanna was doing a good job, moving the raft quickly toward midriver, and Fargo's eyes flicked to the distant top of the high lake. Nugget would have seen the raft push from shore by now. He'd be at the spill gate, starting to get it open. Fargo swore silently, his hope an ironic one. He'd never before wanted an order not to be carried out.

Kale came forward with a quick step and swung, and Fargo parried the blow and returned his own. Kale was a fraction slow in reacting and the blade glanced off an arm. Fargo saw Kale wince as he pulled back. Again Fargo let his eyes flick to the high lake. There was still no sign of anything. He grunted gratefully and stepped toward Kale, this time carrying the broadax waist-high, ready to smash in any direction with it. Kale feinted, drew back when Fargo refused to be drawn off-balance.

Fargo swore under his breath and wondered how many seconds were left. He came at Kale, moved fast and let Kale swing his broadax. He started to parry the blow, then pulled back, and Kale came forward off-balance. Fargo swung, his ax a quick, arching motion. Kale managed to twist away, but not fast enough to avoid the side of the ax striking him in the face. He went sprawling but kept hold of his weapon as he landed in the center of the raft. He started to turn and Fargo saw that one of his long sideburns was matted with red. He wasn't dazed, but he was very much slowed, and Fargo went for him, lifting the heavy broadax.

He was going at Kale, who had only managed to pull himself onto one knee, when he caught the movement from his left and turned to see Joanna charging at him, the pointed hook of the pole held out in front of her as though it were a lance. He tried to halt, stumbled and tried to twist away, but he felt the pointed hook tear through his shirt and the pain of torn flesh exploded. The hook had ripped a path across the skin and his midsection and he felt the instant flow of warm liquid even as he stuck out his foot and Joanna went stumbling in front of him. She sprawled on the logs of the raft, the hooked pole still in her hands, and Fargo saw Duncan Kale had regained his feet again.

The man came at him swinging his weapon, but Fargo easily ducked the blow. He sent his own blade in a horizontal, slicing arc, felt it smash into Kale's ribs. "Oh, Jesus," Kale groaned as he staggered backward. The ax fell from his hand as he sank to the floor of the raft. Fargo saw Joanna, the hooked pole in her hands, on her feet again, her eyes on Kale, who held one hand to his side as a stream of red poured from his ribs.

The sound came then, a tremendous cracking first, as though the world were splitting open. A thunderous roar followed at once and Fargo turned to look up at the high lake. The huge logs were spilling out, carried downward on the cascading torrent of water. The splash was a roar that sent towering sprays of water into the air, a diaphanous white veil that obscured the tumbling logs for a moment. But the huge spray settled back and now the logs were hurtling into the river, a tremendous, foaming wall of water rushing ahead of them. Fargo stared at the terrifying spectacle—the onrushing, boiling water, the hurtling logs, some still turning end over end.

His arms hanging loosely, the ax still in one hand, he turned to see Duncan Kale behind him, on his feet, stumbling forward with his broadax upraised as his side ran red. Kale swung his weapon, using both hands to do so, a last desperate blow. Fargo easily dropped low as the ax passed over his head. His reaction was reflex, no planning in it, hardly even intent, but he swung his broadax, saw the blade smash into Duncan Kale's knees. The man dropped with a gasped cry of pain, collapsed in a heap with both knees shattered pieces of bone and trails of blood. Joanna fell to her knees beside him, caught his head in her arms as he started to fall backward.

Fargo swore as he turned to look back and saw the mountain of onrushing water and hurtling timber racing toward them. The roar intensified, its sound filling the air, and as far as he could see, the gargantuan logs jammed together, crushing anything in their path. They were but seconds away now and he flung the ax down as he halted, poised at the edge of the raft.

"Leave him!" he shouted at Joanna. "Come on, jump!" But Joanna didn't even turn her head as she cradled Duncan Kale in her arms, rocking his broken body back and forth. Fargo used another precious second. "It's over. You can't help him. Jump, for God's sake!" he shouted. But Joanna Petersen only continued to rock back and forth. He thought he heard her humming but he wasn't sure. The hissing, roaring sound was deafening now. Fargo saw the logs rise up in front of him, a great, wild beast of lumber, rearing up with a thousand legs to stomp him to bits.

He dived from the raft, arching his body so he'd have

as much downward thrust as possible as he cleaved the water. He felt the water close around him as he frantically propelled himself down deeper, and then suddenly the hurtling logs were passing over him. He felt the water spin him, pull him around, swirl him in huge underwater eddies of turbulence. The sweeping fury of the logs had smashed into the raft by now, he knew, upending it and smashing it to smithereens. He didn't waste precious strength or breath tring to fight the swirling currents that pulled him one way and then another, but a terrible realization stabbed into him.

The logs would take minutes to pass over him, even at their onrushing pace, a ceiling of timber without an inch of space in it. His breath would never hold out long enough. He could already feel the tightness growing in his chest. The undercurrent continued to sweep him along and the tightness was becoming a burning pain. He turned onto his back and he could see the dark ceiling above him, unbroken and seemingly endless.

Suddenly he was whirled sideways, a surge of current pulling at him. He'd no strength left to fight against it and his lungs were on fire. The current continued to pull him to the side and suddenly he was bumping against mud, his feet touching bottom. He was against the shore and he glimpsed a narrow strip of the surface water where he could see daylight. He propelled himself upward with the last of his remaining strength and the narrow strip remained, beckoning, almost mocking. He reached it and burst through the surface, his mouth opening to gulp in deep drafts of air. He reached out with one arm, clung to the soft soil of the shoreline, and heard the logs thundering past him, smashing each other as they raced downriver.

But the curve of the river bottom held them racing with a space, less than a foot, from the edge of the shore. He lay there with his breath coming in labored gasps, his lungs beginning to return to something approaching normalcy, and he gave thanks for miracles. But his legs still quivered and the weakness was still upon him. He lay still, his cheek pressed against the cool softness of the shore's sandy soil while, less than twelve inches behind him, the logs continued to hurtle past. But he was alive, half on shore and alive. A damn miracle, he told himself again. "I'm alive," he muttered aloud, wanting to hear the words to make sure he wasn't in the half-world of the newly dead. "I'm alive."

"*Not for long,*" a voice answered him, and he grimaced into the sand. Maybe he wasn't alive. Maybe it was all a last dream. "*I'm going to kill you,*" he heard the voice say, a sepulchral whisper. He forced his eyes open and lifted his head, staring into the sun. The figure standing but a foot away from him took shape.

"My God," Fargo breathed as Joanna took a step closer. Her clothes, soaked, clung to her voluptuous body, but her hair was matted against her head and one side of her face was a torn red smear. Her shirt was ripped away from one shoulder and he saw the deep, dripping gash that went halfway down her arm. Her eyes were wild and staring and her lips drawn back, her mouth half open. She could have been a creature risen from hell, he found himself thinking. But a creature with half the pole in one hand, the half with the sharp, hooked end.

He stared up at her as he realized what had happened. Somehow, when the raft upended, she had been flung clear, thrown onto one of the onrushing logs and then flung into the air again. She had landed in the water but close enough to that narrow space along the shore and somehow she had managed to keep hold of the broken pole. And now she held it raised to plunge into him. Not all miracles were good ones, he thought grimly.

"You killed Duncan," Joanna hissed.

Fargo shook his head and his hand opened against the soil. But there was still little strength in him, he realized. "No, you killed him," he told her. He wanted to buy precious seconds. He felt the trembling in his legs stop. "You wanted that, only you didn't. You should've made up your mind long ago," he said, hurling harshness at her. She took another step forward and the hooked end of the pole was raised high now. She'd run him through with it, pin him to the ground the way a butterfly is pinned by a collector. He felt strength flowing back through his body with frustrating slowness. He still wouldn't have the speed to roll aside fast enough to avoid the tearing hook. She was an avenging goddess, ready to impale her enemy, consumed with an awful purpose.

He had to make that crack open. He had to get her to explode with fury and make a mistake. He had to replace her dead-cold poise with rage. "Duncan was nothing," Fargo said. "Small shit. He cheated, lied, and stole to get what he wanted. But you killed to get what you wanted. You had a good, innocent girl gunned down and almost killed another. You're a big-time bitch, honey. But stupid."

Joanna's mouth fell open as she let out a piercing scream of fury. She could have flung the pole through him from where she was, but she leaped forward to plunge it into him again and again. She had cracked and made her mistake, and he had that precious split second he needed. He flung his arm out, smashed it across her ankles as she

162

came in, and she stumbled and lost her balance just as she came down with the pole. He saw the hooked and pointed end plunge into the soil a half-inch from his face as Joanna fell forward on both knees.

She spun and dived for the pole but he was pulling it from the ground with both hands. He rolled with it, had it in front of him as she flung herself at him screaming. It all happened too fast for him to turn the pole away and he felt the shock run through his arms as she impaled herself on it. Her mouth opened again but the scream was soundless this time as she hung over him, the pole deep into her abdomen.

He took his hands from the end of the pole and Joanna fell alongside him, and he pushed to his feet to see the point of the pole sticking out through her back. Her eyes were open, staring at him, the hatred still in them. "For Evie," he said as he turned and walked away, hearing her last shuddered gasp.

He walked along the riverbank, the last of the logs passing him, and realized the raft had traveled more than a quarter-mile from the camp. When he finally reached the logging camp he saw the small knots of subdued figures still in clusters, still trying to assimilate all that had exploded in their faces. But then he saw the slender figure racing across the ground toward him, curly brown hair flying in the wind. She catapulted herself into his arms, clung to him with her arms and legs wrapped around him.

"Oh, God, oh, God," she breathed. "I thought you were dead."

"I told you, that's been rumored before," he said as she slid her feet to the ground to peer up at him, disbelief and joy mixing in her face.

"I saw you go after him and I ran from the tent to help.

But you jumped onto the raft before I could reach you," Glory said. "And then, when the splash came . . . Oh, God, I knew it was all over." A shudder went through her as she recalled the moment. "Why did it happen then? Everything just break open at the wrong moment?"

"Yes and no." He smiled and she frowned back. He saw the white thatch of hair appear from the other end of the camp and move toward him, and waited as the old miner came to a halt.

"How'd I do?" Nugget asked.

"You did fine, just fine," Fargo said with a smile.

"Would someone like to explain all this to me?" Glory cut in.

"I will while we're going back," he said. "Get your things together." She nodded and hurried off toward the tent, and Fargo saw Gus Harby watching him, uncertainty in the man's face. "It's over," Fargo told him. "All over." Harby continued to look uncertain. "You were a hired hand," Fargo said. "You followed orders. I've no quarrel with you." The man nodded and Fargo saw the relief slide across his face as he walked on. Fargo's eyes turned to Nugget. "You coming back with us?" he asked.

"No," Nugget said. "I'm not going back to being a town drunk and I never liked towns much, anyway. The cook's a good man. I think I'll stay here awhile, find a new life for myself. Might even do some mining again."

Fargo nodded. "Let's go get my gun," he said as he started toward the cook's wagon.

"You let me come along. You'd faith in me and it broke that chain for me. I'll never forget that, Fargo," Nugget said.

"Maybe I gave you a chance, but you had to break the

chain yourself, old-timer.'' Fargo smiled as he clasped Nugget's outstretched hand.

The cook returned the Colt and the gunbelt to Fargo, and he'd just strapped it on when Glory appeared leading the Ovaro and her roan. He swung onto the pinto as she said good-bye to Nugget. Minutes later she rode beside him as he led the way from the logging camp.

''You were right about Evie all along,'' he said. ''Joanna was behind it.''

''My God,'' Glory breathed.

''I've a lot to tell you,'' Fargo said.

''All right, but you've a lot more than talking to do,'' Glory said, and he saw the little smile that flickered across her face. Her eyes met his glance, as saucy as the upturned line of her breasts.

''Damn right,'' he agreed. ''Damn right.'' Glory's little smile took on satisfaction. He found himself smiling back. The trip back would be a lot more pleasurable than the one out. Damn right, he told himself again.

LOOKING FORWARD!

**The following is the opening
section from the next novel in the exciting
Trailsman series from Signet:**

THE TRAILSMAN #122
GOLD FEVER

*Autumn, 1859—the Rocky Mountains,
where gold was king,
greed and gunfights flourished,
and bullets were dirt-cheap.*

"You sure are having a peculiar string of luck, stranger," commented the crusty prospector in the battered black hat, his flinty eyes on the big man in buckskins seated directly across from him at the poker table.

Idly studying the five cards in his left hand, Skye Fargo could almost feel the tension that suddenly gripped the other players and the patrons of the Concert Hall who were observing the game. One of the premier gambling establishments in the year-old town, the Concert Hall enjoyed booming business thanks to the hordes of gold seekers who were flocking west from the states in the hopes of striking it rich in the nearby Rocky Mountains. Several fantastic finds had been made earlier in the year and duly mentioned in every newspaper east of the Mississippi River, luring a steady stream of gold-hungry humanity into the region.

Fargo had ridden into Denver several years ago, intent on treating himself to a little relaxation after completing a dangerous scouting mission for the Army in Ute country. And now he was two hours into a game of stud poker that had seen his stake grow from thirty to one hundred and ten dollars, a feat the prospector had foolishly seen fit to question. Fargo's lake-blue eyes narrowed as he regarded the speaker coldly. "Are you saying I cheat?" he demanded.

The three other players all wore expressions indicating they would rather be anywhere than where they were. Not a one so much as blinked.

Stiffening in resentment, the prospector pushed his hat back on his head. He opened his mouth to say something, then looked deep into Fargo's eyes and apparently thought better of the notion. "No, I reckon not," he said softly.

The other players relaxed. One of the spectators expelled a sigh of relief.

A melodious female voice abruptly spoke up from behind Fargo. "A man should always watch what he says. Hot words, often as not, lead to a cold grave."

Hands fell on Fargo's shoulders, and he twisted to find the lovely woman who oversaw the gambling end of the operations at the Concert Hall, a feisty blond named Lacy Dalton. Rumor had it that she had once been the owner's mistress, and the man had rewarded her affection by giving her the lucrative position. During the evening and nighttime hours she frequently made the rounds of the poker, faro, and keno tables, making jokes and letting the men admire her shapely figure, invariably sheathed in a lacy red dress. Her green eyes focused on the prospector as she leaned forward and said, "Do you have a complaint to lodge, Mr. Turner?"

"No, ma'am," Turner promptly responded.

"I heard what you said," Lacy noted sternly. "And I'll tell you that you're making a big mistake if you think Skye Fargo would stoop so low as to cheat at any game."

The prospector began raking in the few dollars in coins lying in front of him. "I didn't mean nothing, honest. I guess I've had too much to drink, is all." He stood and stuffed the money into a pocket of his well-worn pants. "Now I'll just mosey along and get sober."

"Aren't you going to finish out this hand?" the player on his right asked.

"I'm about tapped out," Turner said. "You boys finish without me." So saying, he spun on his heels and hastened off.

"Strange," Lacy remarked. "He usually doesn't back down so easily. I figured for sure he would make a scene."

Fargo placed his cards on the table, facedown. "Know him well, do you?"

"Not really. He's been in here a dozen times in the past month or so, and he always winds up in an argument with somebody or other. Bitter man, I reckon. He went out to California in forty-nine and about lost his shirt. Now he's desperate to locate a rich vein hereabouts."

"Him and forty thousand other pilgrims," Fargo noted, watching the prospector depart. The man hadn't been toting a firearm, but he had the feeling Turner could be a dangerous hombre when aroused. Every instinct told him to keep one eye over his shoulder from now on. Some men, and Turner might be just the type, didn't take too kindly to being made to back down in public. There was no telling what Turner might do.

Lacy gave Fargo's shoulders an affectionate squeeze. "When you're done here, I'll let you buy me a drink again."

"You're on," Fargo said, and resumed playing as she sashayed toward the long mahogany bar fronting the north wall. The enticing sway of her hips caused a stirring in his loins, and he imagined how she would look without that red dress on. The night before he'd shared a few drinks with her and made small talk for half an hour or so, but nothing had come of it. Maybe tonight would be different.

The card game continued for a dozen more hands. Only Fargo and one other man were still in when Fargo asked for two cards and was dealt an eight and a jack. He already held a pair of eights and a five, and he barely suppressed a grin at his good luck. The pot, he noticed, stood at thirty dollars.

"It's your bet," the player said.

"Let's make this interesting," Fargo said, counting out forty dollars and adding the money to the pile.

The other man, a lean fellow in a drab suit, also took two cards. He studied his hand for a bit, licking his thin lips all the while, and stated, "I'll see you, and raise you another fifty." He proceeded to do so, using hasty, nervous movements.

Was he bluffing? Fargo wondered, and decided to find out. "I'll call," he said, putting in the fifty. "Let's see what you've got, mister."

The thin man beamed triumphantly. "A full house," he announced, and proudly displayed three kings and two queens.

Fargo threw down his hand in disgust. So much for good luck! He picked up the fifteen dollars he had left and stood. "Thanks for the game, gents," he said, turning toward the bar, thankful he'd paid for his room at the Dutchman Hotel in advance. As it was, after he purchased the few supplies he needed, he'd ride out of Denver practically broke.

There was no sign of Lacy Dalton. Fargo ordered a whiskey and stood with his left elbow propped on the bar top, sipping slowly. It would be his last drink for a spell and he wanted to savor it.

A red figure materialized among the packed patrons, and Lacy came strolling in his direction. "Don't tell me," she said, smirking. "The look on your face says it all. You're cleaned out."

"Close, but not quite," Fargo admitted, and shrugged. "I wasn't cut out to be a gambler." He motioned for the barkeep and asked her, "Do you want the same as last night?"

"No brandy this time," Lacy said. "I'm off tomorrow, so I can drink the hard stuff if I want. Give me what you're having."

Fargo ordered, and after the barkeep moved off he let his gaze rove over her voluptuous thighs and full bosom. The tight dress caused her ample breasts to bulge as if about to burst from the garment.

"Like what you see?" she inquired in a teasing tone.

"A man would have to be made of stone not to," Fargo answered, and gulped some whiskey.

"How would you like the honor of walking me home tonight?"

"I'll carry you if you want."

Laughter rippled from her rosy lips and she shook her head. "That won't be necessary, thank you. But I'd feel safer with a rugged man like you along. There are so many footpads and other hardcases abroad at night that it's not smart to go anywhere alone.'' She glanced at the Colt snug in its holster on his right hip. ''I bet you're quite handy with that hog-leg.''

''I've been known to hit what I aim at,'' Fargo allowed. He didn't bother to brag that he could draw and hit a target the size of a small coin in the time it would take her to blink. Nor did he mention he carried a throwing knife, a razor-sharp Arkansas toothpick, in a sheath in his right boot.

Lacy moved closer until their arms were touching. ''I'm looking forward to this, handsome. I hope you won't disappoint me.''

''I'll do my best,'' Fargo promised.

''Let's drink to that,'' Lacy proposed, raising her glass.

Lifting his own, Fargo heard a commotion break out in the crowd to his right. There were low cries and the sound of running feet. He pivoted, his right hand resting on the bar, more curious than concerned.

''Another move and you're dead, card cheat!''

Ten feet away stood the prospector named Turner, a shotgun in his hands, the twin barrels leveled at Fargo's abdomen.

Complete silence descended on the spacious, elegant gaming room. Those nearest Turner fearfully moved away from him. Everyone else wisely froze.

''I want the money you took from me, you bastard!'' Turner bellowed. ''If you don't hand it over, I'll blow you in half.''

Fargo saw the man sway slightly and realized Turner had done more drinking since leaving the game. His gut involuntarily tightened. Drunks were ten times as deadly as sober men because they were more likely to cut loose at the least little provocation and didn't give a tinker's damn about who might be caught in a cross fire. And a shotgun only compounded the problem; if loaded with buckshot, it sprayed out lethal lead in a wide pattern. He knew if Turner fired, Lacy and those on either side would also die. Keeping his voice as calm as possible, he said, "I don't have your money. I lost it all after you left." As he spoke, he carefully lowered his whiskey to the counter.

Turner took a step and wagged the shotgun in a menacing gesture. "What do you take me for, a greenhorn?"

"Please, Mr. Turner," Lacy interjected, her glass still held high. "This is no way to be acting. Put that shotgun down and let's talk this over."

"Shut your mouth, whore," the prospector snapped. "I seen the way you were looking at this son of a bitch. You're sweet on him." He sneered. "So I reckon it's only fitting that both of you go out together."

"It's the money you want," Fargo reminded him. "Let her walk away. This is just between you and me."

Turner straightened, his brow knit in thought. "Yeah, I don't want to be known as no woman killer." He bent his head to the right. "Move over that way, out of the line of fire. The rest of you do the same."

The patrons at the bar eagerly complied, all except for Lacy. She slowly stepped to one side, her hand, oddly, still elevated.

"Now I can settle my score with you," Turner told Fargo, and tucked the shotgun stock to his right shoulder, about to take deliberate aim.

Fargo tensed, prepared to make a desperate bid for his revolver, not about to go down without a fight, although even if he tied Turner he was dead. The blast from that double-barreled cannon would rip him to ribbons and no doctor in the world would be able to sew him back together.

Turner cackled. "I'll teach you to trifle with me, sidewinder."

The moment of truth had arrived. Fargo had no choice but to streak his right hand to his Colt, but even as he did an unexpected occurrence gave him a fleeting edge. A loud noise, that of glass shattering against the bar, diverted Turner's attention for all of one second. The prospector glanced at the source a heartbeat before his finger started to squeeze the outer trigger. Fargo saw the man's eyes flick back toward him as he brought the .44 up and out, and he fired two shots in swift succession.

Turner's dulled senses were unequal to the occasion. The slugs caught him high in the chest, making him stagger rearward, the shotgun drooping in his limp arms. He managed to get off a shot, the buckshot tearing a gaping hole in the floor, the recoil knocking the weapon from his hands. Tottering, he clutched at the crimson bullet holes, staining his fingers red with his own blood, and then pitched onto his face with a dull thud.

No one spoke. No one moved.

Fargo held the Colt at waist height and walked over to the prospector. A brief check verified the man was dead. Frowning, he slid the .44 into the holster and gazed at Lacy. She was leaning on the bar, her glass lying in fragments to her left.

"Much obliged," he said.

"It was all I could think of."

"I owe you," Fargo said. Another commotion erupted and he shifted to see three men in fine suits shoving their way through the gawking crowd, revolvers in their hands.

"It's all right, boys," Lacy called out. "One of the customers got a mite rowdy. Drag his carcass out of here and let the law know." She ambled over to Fargo and looped her arm in his. "Don't worry none about the marshal. Everyone here saw you shoot in self-defense." Her voice dropped to a whisper. "Besides, we pay him five hundred a month to look the other way whenever there's trouble."

The three men were all business as two grabbed Turner by the heels and commenced dragging him off while the third picked up the shotgun and trailed along. Murmuring broke out among the customers, with many an awed glance cast in the Trailsman's direction.

"By tomorrow everyone in Denver will know about the shooting," Lacy said.

"Yep," Fargo responded, looking at a smear of blood marking the spot where Turner had fallen. There was a possibility the prospector might have friends who would seek revenge, and he had no intention of staying around to be their target. Tomorrow afternoon he would cut out. It was high time, anyway. He missed the wide open spaces, the prairies, mountains, and woodlands he called his home.

BLAZING NEW TRAILS
WITH SKYE FARGO